DONNA JO NAPOLI

Lights on the Nile

HARPER

An Imprint of HarperCollinsPublishers

Library of Congress Cataloging-in-Publication Data
Napoli, Donna Jo, date
    Lights on the Nile / Donna Jo Napoli
        p.   cm.
    Summary: Ten-year-old Kepi, a young girl in ancient Egypt,
embarks on a journey to save her family when she is unexpectedly
taken captive, along with the baby baboon she has rescued from a
crocodile. An origin tale about fairies.
    ISBN 978-0-06-166793-0 (trade bdg.)
    [1. Kidnapping—Fiction.   2. Egypt—History—To 332 B.C.—
Fiction.   3. Baboons—Fiction.   4. Fairies—Fiction.]   I. Title
PZ7.N15Lh   2011
[Fic]—dc22   2011010179
                                                               CIP
                                                                AC

11 12 13 14 15   CG/RRDB   10 9 8 7 6 5 4 3 2 1
❖
First Edition

To the memory of my grandmother,
born in Alexandria

CONTENTS

ACKNOWLEDGMENTS

Thanks to Barry and Elena Furrow; Jenna Beucler; Sarah Flint; Nicholas Gaw; Libby Crissey; Katherine Delaney; Serafina Hilliard; Ben Hunter; Tim Jensen; Courtney Knerr; Lena Lofgren; David McKay; Daniel, Donna, Emily, Kelly, and Timothy McKenna; Tatum Murray; Abigail Raz; Jill Stengel; Kevin Stern; Nate Urban; Morgan Wesley; Ed Gaynor's fourth-grade class at the Swarthmore-Rutledge school in fall 2008; and the one who asked me about Tinker Bell in the first place, my dear Brenda Bowen. Finally, a huge thank-you to Jordan Brown, who never tires, even when the task tests all our strength.

Note to the Reader

This story takes place in ancient Egypt around 2530 BCE, near the end of the rule of Pharaoh Khufu.

1

CLICK

Kepi looked down at the beetle that crawled across her knuckles. The two spots on its back seemed to glow. And its head was tiny. She was pretty sure of what it was.

"Kepi! Again?"

Kepi's eyes jumped to her mother, standing at the end of the bean row, and just as thin as a bean plant herself.

Mother glared at her. "Do I have to scold you every five minutes to keep you moving? Every job matters. The god Osiris watches as we do our fieldwork. He's watching you. . . ."

Mother kept talking. Blah blah blah. Everything was sacred to her. That's all she cared about, sacred this, sacred that. Who really knew when the god Osiris was watching? Kepi bet he never watched. At least not their family. And maybe fieldwork wasn't on Kepi's right path, anyway.

Besides, the afterlife was far away. But this beetle was here. And it was special—she could have bet on that. Kepi smiled.

"I see that smile! That's the naughty smile of someone shirking her work."

"I'm not shirking my work."

"Silly," came Nanu's voice. Her round face poked up over a bean plant from the next row over. "You're goofing off, little liar."

"What's that?" Mother now stood over Kepi. She leaned close and her long, thin nose almost touched Kepi's shoulder. "A beetle! Kill it fast."

Kepi instantly cradled her right hand to her chest and clapped her left hand over it. "It's sacred."

Mother pursed her lips.

Ha! That stopped her.

"Are you sure? Let's be sure."

Kepi opened her hands, and the beetle crawled up her left arm. She plucked it off and set it on its back in the dirt. The beetle's stick legs worked the air furiously.

"See?" Kepi pointed at the shiny spot on its tummy. "It's a click beetle."

Just then the beetle arched its back and *click!* It flipped into the air so high, it hit Kepi between the eyes. It landed on its feet and scurried in among the bean vines.

Mother rubbed her hand over her mouth in worry. "It's going to lay eggs."

"Then there will be more beetles," said Kepi happily.

"Idiot," said Nanu. "Beetle larvae eat plant roots. We will have carried all those heavy water buckets for nothing."

"Catch it quick," said Mother.

"But it's sacred, I told you. The goddess Nit protects it. Father says."

At the mention of Kepi's father, Mother's face went soft. "Then don't kill it. Catch it and take it far before you let it go."

Kepi wouldn't have killed the beetle anyway. She could never kill anything, no matter what Mother ordered. But she nodded obediently. "How far?"

"Beyond the fields. All of them."

Kepi bowed her head so her mother couldn't see her smile.

"No fair." Nanu stood up and brushed her long pigtails back over her shoulders. "If she gets to go off on a walk, I get to rest till she comes back."

"Carrying this beetle away from our crops isn't resting," said Mother.

"It's a lot easier than lugging a water bucket."

"I've been cursed with two shiftless daughters." Mother shook her head ruefully. "How can your father and I ever count on you taking care of us in our old age if you act so lazy?"

Nanu kicked Kepi. Kepi leaped to her feet beside her older sister. Together they said, "You're not old yet." It was a practiced chorus. They'd said it dozens of times in the past two months. Since their father had come home injured, it seemed all Mother thought about was her old age.

Mother looked off, her lips pursed again. Then her shoulders slumped. "Oh, all right. Nanu, help me in the house till Kepi returns. Go now, Kepi. Catch that beetle. Remember, be careful not to hurt it. We mustn't incur the wrath of the goddess. We have enough trouble. Don't talk to anyone. Keep your eyes lowered and move fast." She walked back down the bean row.

Kepi looked around. "Little beetle, little beetle, where did you go?"

"You actually like that bug," said Nanu in Kepi's ear. "That makes you creepy."

"If you don't like bugs, why do you wear that bone amulet? It's shaped like a scarab."

"Scarabs are pretty. Click beetles are gross." Nanu looked Kepi in the eye now, serious. "And you better really catch it and not just lie and say you did. We're poor now that Father can't plow the fields anymore. We need all our crops to pay the men who plowed for us.

If we lose our land, it'll be your fault." She turned and followed Mother. Her copper bracelets clinked against one another as she walked. She stopped a moment, and without looking back, she shimmied both hands so that her bracelets sent up the most beautiful tinkling noise.

Kepi touched her own bare wrists, bare neck. She looked down at her bare ankles. Everyone else her age and even much younger wore jewelry constantly, no matter whether they were poor or rich. Father said that was one of the wonderful things about people in Egypt. But Kepi had the awful habit of losing things, so Mother had decided she should go without jewelry when she worked in the fields. It was unfair. Kepi didn't try to lose things—it just happened.

And it was specially unfair because Kepi was the one who loved to make that tinkling noise, not Nanu. When Mother first said Kepi couldn't wear jewelry in the fields, Kepi waited for moonlight, then prayed with all her heart to the goddess Hathor. She'd prayed, *Please, great goddess Hathor, please make my mother change her mind and let me wear jewelry into the fields.* Father said Hathor wore a wonderful necklace, a *menat*, that made the best noise when she danced—everyone loved that noise. Kepi wanted to sound like that; she wanted everyone to love the noise she made.

But the goddess Hathor was just like all the other

gods; she didn't listen to Kepi's prayers. And Father never won against her mother. So Mother's decree held: no jewelry in the fields for Kepi. She sighed.

Well, at least she had hair. Most girls her age had a shaved head. But when Nanu had become old enough to grow her hair, Kepi had begged Mother to let her, too. And after months of begging, she'd won.

And at least she didn't go naked anymore. Her dress was a simple sheath that covered her from armpits to knees, with wide straps over the shoulders. She loved it.

Kepi fell to her knees, searching among the bean vines, lifting leaves gingerly. The new vines could snap if she was rough. She peeked at the underside of every leaf. How much damage could a single beetle do? Would her family really lose their land? No farmers in their village were rich, but at least they always had food. How would Kepi's family feed themselves if they lost their land?

Kepi chewed on the tip of a lock of hair. She blew through her lips in worry, making a blubbery sound.

An idea came. Kepi made her lips firm and blew through them hard, right up at the bean vines. Then she sat back on her heels to listen. And—*click!* Yes, the noise came from a little to her right. *Thank you, goddess Nit,* prayed Kepi. *Thank you for letting me find your beetle.*

Ua. The noise wavered, like a voice under water. Kepi

touched her ears and looked around, but she saw no one. That was strange. She had heard a noise for sure; she hadn't just imagined it.

Mother had taught Kepi and Nanu to thank the gods for anything good that happened. She said the gods would do horrible things if you didn't. Kepi didn't like that idea. If you prayed to the gods, they might very well ignore you—she knew that too well. But if you didn't thank the gods, they would punish you. What was fair about that? Still, Kepi gave thanks, even though she figured no one was listening.

But now she'd heard something. A word.

Or maybe it was nothing. A wind noise. Kepi shook her head and leaned over the beetle.

2
BABOON

Carefully Kepi cupped the beetle in her hands and walked along the canal that was connected to the river.

The soft ground got even softer as she left the bean field and approached the Nile. All the land that the Nile flooded was black earth, rich with river silt. But the land closest to the banks was the richest. Slender flax plants were set close together here to make them grow tall. Anyone could harvest flax; all you had to do was pull it up by the roots. It wasn't like wheat or barley; those had to be cut with heavy sickles, so only men could do it. After the next full moon Kepi would join Nanu and Mother in harvesting the first flax, it grew so fast. And she'd pull even more flax after the second planting, for flax was a winter plant. When the flax was finished, Mother would be sure to find Kepi something else to do; their family always planted three times before the floods came again.

She gave another sigh. Life had turned into so much work. It had been more fun being a little kid. But Mother needed all the help she could get, and Kepi was ten now.

She went along the riverbank, going the opposite way of the current, until all the fields were behind her. Then she kept walking. Click beetles didn't travel far; they didn't fly except at night, and then only within their territory. Kepi knew this because her father had taught her. During the three to four months every year when the Nile would flood and farmers had no work, Father took her exploring in the countryside. They'd be gone for weeks at a time, sleeping in huts they made from palm fronds. Nanu never liked exploring, but Kepi loved it, so it was just Father and Kepi. Kepi knew lots about the animals and plants of the floodplain and the desert. And at night, under the palm fronds, Father would tell Kepi stories of the gods. Mother might be the one who taught Nanu and Kepi what would happen to them if they didn't obey the gods, but Father was the one who knew all the tales about them.

Best of all, for the last few years Kepi had managed to tame a wild animal on each adventure. Not fully tame— not turn them into pets. But rather, Kepi would make friends with a creature just enough that she could feed it from her hand. Usually birds—a cute hoopoe with a little striped tuft on its head, a kestrel with glorious red and blue feathers, even a Nile goose, despite their usual bad temper. Once she found a mongoose, sleek and long with that elegant tapered snout. Kepi remembered every detail about every one of them.

Whenever Mother complained that Father and Kepi had wasted time out in the wild, Father said, "If you're searching for a *neter*, a god—observe nature." That always made Mother hush. Nothing was better than those days and nights with Father.

But all that was over, for Father would never take Kepi exploring again. She swallowed a lump in her throat at the painful thought. Pharaoh Khufu was building another pyramid, even taller than the three his father, Pharaoh Sneferu, had built. Five months ago, when the Nile waters rose, her father had been offered a tax waiver if he would work on a barge carrying the huge granite blocks from Upper Egypt, where they were quarried, all the way north to the delta of the Nile for the inner chamber of the new grand pyramid. This was the same offer Father had gotten every year. Usually Father said no and, instead, paid his taxes in extra grain. This year, though, he'd accepted the offer. He had wanted to keep all his harvest so that he could trade other farmers for additional land. Nanu was twelve now, and it was time to marry her off—and a woman should have land of her own as security when she entered a marriage.

But the very first week their father had arrived up north, a chunk of limestone fell on him and crushed one leg from the knee down. The pharaoh's surgeon had straightened Father's lower leg bones and made him a cast from cow milk and ground barley glued together with tree gum. But Father's foot was the problem. The open wound wouldn't heal, no matter how much cow dung the surgeon put on it. It festered until the surgeon had to cut it off and finally sent him back.

Father still suffered pain. He worked only at home now, seated in front of the large stone mortar. He grasped the pestle in both hands and pounded grain for hours as if in a fury until it formed the finest powder. It was grain from last year—so it was old and musty. Nevertheless, neighbors who tasted bread made from it said it was the best ever.

So Kepi's father was always busy and never lonely. But he was also always at home. Stuck.

At least he could make a little bit of money for the family as a baker, so long as they had their own grain from their own land. It was a good thing Kepi had spotted this click beetle. If she saw others, she had to carry them far away, too. Beetles mustn't ruin their crops. It was important that her father never have to sell their land.

But it was clear Father would never make enough money to buy extra land for Nanu now. She could get married with or without owning her own property, of course. But if the marriage didn't work out, Nanu might want to leave her husband. If she had her own land, she could farm it or sell it. Either way, she could take care of herself. But without her own land, what would happen to her?

All this worry. Their family never used to worry.

It was all Pharaoh Khufu's fault. Now Father had to pay others to plow his land and help in the harvest, and he still had to pay his taxes every year. It was too unfair. Pharaoh Khufu shouldn't ask Father for taxes anymore. *He* should give *Father* money—not the other way around. Pharaoh Khufu should take better care of his people.

Kepi hated Pharaoh Khufu. It was wrong to hate the pharaoh. Dangerous, even. He was a god in his own way, after all. But Kepi couldn't help it. If she ever got the chance, she'd tell him off, all right. Someone had to take care of her family. The pharaoh wasn't doing it, and the gods sure weren't either.

Father wasn't happy anymore. Mother wasn't happy anymore. Nanu wasn't happy anymore. How could Kepi be happy? A feeling like tiny cold feet raced across her shoulders.

Kepi raised her cupped hands to her eyes and peeked through her fingers at the treasure within. "How did you ever get to our field, little click beetle? Were you exploring? Don't you know it's dangerous to go that far alone?"

She stepped up her pace now. Kepi herself had never strayed this far alone before. It had taken so long to get here that it would be dark by the time she made it back home. That meant they wouldn't be able to work anymore today. And that meant she had gone far enough. Kepi wasn't really trying to shirk work, just to put it off a little while. It was a pity that broad beans were so thirsty all the time. They were as bad as chicory and lettuce. In fact, most crops demanded watering all the time. Only the grapes and grains weren't greedy.

Kepi blinked at her own thoughts. When she said things like this aloud, Mother would answer that the god Set was watching her. Mother said that the god Set often watched her. Set was the god of storms, and Kepi's name meant "tempest"—so, according to Mother, Set's eye was on her. Lettuce was Set's favorite food. It was not a good idea to say bad things about lettuce, even inside your own head. Set could be vengeful. Mother had a list of vengeful gods, and Set was among the worst.

There was a stand of date palms ahead. The click beetle would be happy among the trees. Kepi ran.

Within moments she heard grunts. She was amazed, for she recognized those rhythmic noises. Most people from Egypt wouldn't. But Kepi had traveled south with Father into Nubian lands, so she knew animals her neighbors had never seen. She stopped dead and squatted, curling her shoulders forward as tight as possible.

It wasn't just the one grunter—no, no, a whole troop of baboons came dropping out of the date palms and went romping away on all fours. The bigger one had a silver mane, crimped perfectly. There was a dent in the middle of his head, as though someone had bashed him with a thick pole. He was double the size of the others but still shorter than Kepi, even stretched to his tallest. But size wasn't everything; Kepi had seen baboon fangs tear an antelope apart. They could easily tear a child apart.

She put her chin to her chest and clamped her head between her knees and squeezed her eyes shut. She knew she should pray in her heart, but a roar filled her. The only thoughts she could form were *help help please help*.

Gradually the roar faded. Noises from outside her filtered in now. Grunts. They were distant. Faint. Finally even that noise stopped. She dared to lift her head. The last of the baboons' pink bottoms disappeared through an acacia thicket far off.

"Thank you," she whispered. "Whoever helped me, thank you."

Uābt.

Kepi whipped her head around and touched one ear with the back of her hand, then the other. She could have sworn she heard someone call her "pure." But there was no one around.

She straightened upright slowly and walked to the nearest date palm, where she set the click beetle free on the bark.

But, oh, she was wrong: The baboons weren't entirely gone; in the date tree closest to the water was a mother with a tiny black baby clinging to the back of her head. The baby's bright pink face peeked out above the mother's dull one. Some of the mother's whiskers were white against her greenish-brown fur. She must be old. She climbed down slowly and awkwardly, as though she was in pain. Her eyebrows raised, showing a white eyelid above ebony eyes that glittered angrily at Kepi. Her head bobbed.

Kepi lowered her gaze and backed away. She mustn't run or the baboon would chase—Father had taught her that. She searched out of the corner of her eye for something to protect herself with. That was when she saw a slight movement. It was the tip of a muddy log floating near the base of the date tree the baboon was coming down from. But no, it wasn't a log; logs didn't move like that. Instantly Kepi knew. She had to run! "Climb back up, baboon! Climb!" Kepi turned to run, and tripped and fell.

The baboon jumped the final bit from the tree, and made as if to chase Kepi, when the crocodile burst forth and closed its jaws around her hindquarters.

The baboon didn't shriek. She just looked at the crocodile, then looked at Kepi. She ripped at her head, and a black scramble of skinny legs and arms and tail flew through the air.

Kepi caught the baby and ran as the crocodile slipped back into the river with the silent baboon mother in its jaws.

3

HERBS

Kepi put the basket of sesame seeds on the ground beside the large wooden bowl. She carefully pried the baby's fingers loose from her hair and lifted him down.

The little baboon sat on the dirt and looked at her quizzically. He rode on her head constantly unless he was eating, and he'd finished his breakfast of honeyed goat milk just a little while ago, so he couldn't expect to eat again yet, especially not outside. His face seemed to ask what was going on.

Kepi used her most encouraging voice. "Pay attention, sweet Babu."

Babu stared at her, just as though he understood her words.

At first she had called him Acenit, "follower of Nit." She'd chosen the name because the night Kepi had carried the baby baboon home from the river, two whole months ago now, Mother wouldn't allow her to bring him inside. But Kepi changed Mother's mind by convincing her that the goddess Nit had given the baboon to her. After all, the click beetle had led Kepi to the baboon baby. And the beetle was sacred to the goddess Nit. It all made sense, sort of. Enough sense that Mother agreed. And naming the baboon Acenit would be a constant reminder to Mother that the baboon should stay.

Still, the name *Acenit* seemed fancy for such a small baby. So Kepi searched for a better name, but always one that would remind Mother of the gods. She thought of the baboon god, Babi. He hated humans and murdered them on sight, so Kepi could never call her baby baboon that. But *Babu* sounded a lot like *Babi*, and it was fun to say. The name stuck.

"Do what I do, Babu." Kepi dug a hand into the bucket of seeds and threw some into the bowl. Then she looked expectantly at Babu.

Babu's eyes flashed with intelligence. With both hands he threw seeds into the bowl. Kepi nodded. Babu did it again and again. Kepi scooped him into her arms and danced in a circle. Her bracelets and anklets tinkled wonderfully. "You are the smartest little baboon that ever lived."

Thud clunk. Thud clunk. It was the sound of Father hopping up the steps from the cellar. Everyone else had woken with the sun, but now that Father slept alone, he had his own routine. He went to sleep after everyone and got up after everyone.

Kepi missed her father at night. When Father had come home from the north without his foot, it was the end of the hottest time of year, the time when the family slept on the roof, where they could catch whatever breeze might come. But hopping on steps made Father's leg throb hideously. And since there were more steps up to the roof than down to the cool of the shallow storage cellar, he had taken to sleeping alone down there.

Now the sun no longer blistered, and they could sleep inside. But Father had kept his habit of sleeping in the cellar. Kepi couldn't imagine falling asleep without seeing the twinkling of the stars. Even in her and Nanu's room, she saw those twinkles because the windows were so high. A part of each of her ancestors, of each of everyone's ancestors, the *akhu*, lived on as a radiant, shining dot that ascended to the heavens and whirled among the gods. When the lights in the sky twinkled at her, Kepi felt safe.

And the lights of the night sky were beautiful, too. Kepi wished her eyes twinkled like that. But they were plain. Everything about her was plain.

"Good morning, Father," Kepi called. She waved to him, setting her bracelets tinkling. "Mother left bread and beer for you on the table inside."

Father rested on the top step, leaning on his crutch. He looked small. He hunched over these days, and each shoulder was topped by a bony knob, as though his body hung from those two pegs. But it was more than just his thinness and posture; he seemed to have shrunk. "Working already, my little jingle-jangle?"

Kepi smiled and shook her bracelets at him. "I'm doing everything you told me to last night."

"Sweet obedience from my younger daughter? No doubt that's the influence of dipping your hand in the honey jar and suckling that baboon right from your fingers. We should start calling you Kebi—honey—instead of Kepi."

Kepi had always wanted to change her name. Other girls had descriptive names, like Layla, "born at night," or hopeful names, like Nanu, "beautiful." And it had worked on Nanu; everyone looked twice at her. But why would anyone name a child "tempest"?

"Babu made this morning's task fun."

"And how did he do that?"

"Watch." Kepi peeled Babu off her chest and set him on the ground by the basket of sesame seeds again. She gave him a quick nod.

Babu tossed seeds from the basket into the bowl.

"No! Stop!" Father pounded his crutch on the ground as furiously as he pounded the grain every day.

Kepi gasped and snatched at Babu, but the little
baboon jumped to her head on his own. He clung so
tight, she had to hold in a yelp. "Baboons are sacred to
the god Tehuti. You always say that."

Father's face softened. "Sacred but still filthy. Roll
the wheat barrel over here."

Kepi hugged the heavy barrel with her chest as she
rolled it along the bottom rim to her father.

Father took off the lid. "Show me your hands."

Kepi rubbed them on the hem of her dress and held
them out for inspection.

"Put one in."

Kepi swished one hand inside the barrel.

"What do you feel?"

"Grains."

"You don't feel chaff or straw or weeds?"

"No, sir."

"You don't feel stones from the hooves of the cattle
that crushed these grains on the threshing floor? Not
even tiny stones the size of sand?"

"No, sir."

"All evening I picked through these grains with
wooden forks. Half the night I strained them through a
sieve. These grains hold not a speck of grit."

"Yes, Father. You cleaned them far better than Mother
and Nanu used to."

"And this morning I'm going to oil my pestle before I grind so no stone chips off. I've been thinking about it. This way I can grind grain into flour as smooth as clean water, and make bread that doesn't wear away teeth till they rot and fall out."

Kepi thought of the toothless adults she knew. "You are wise, Father."

He nodded. "People who eat my tender bread will be able to smile forever. So we can't have hair and grit from baboon hands in our sesame seeds."

Kepi's eyes widened. "You're going to mix sesame in your breads?"

"Not inside, outside. I'll roll the dough in seeds to form a crust. It'll look special. And I have a special job for you now. Something you two can do together, to help me with my new plan for special bread."

"Babu and me?" Kepi smiled; Father had forgiven them.

"Set up the firewood. Then I'll explain."

Kepi happily stacked the wood in a short row, exactly the way Father had taught her. She lined up the heavy bread molds, shaking her wrists as she worked for the delight of the music her bracelets made. Father would fill the molds with dough, then set them directly on the embers.

"Good. Now, you know that old basket in the main room?"

"The one with the hole?"

"Not any longer. I repaired it. It's for you and Babu to fill each day. Today you're to collect wild coriander."

"For your bread? Coriander bread?" Kepi wrinkled her nose. "Whoever heard of such a thing?"

"Rich city folk." Father raised and lowered his eyebrows and made a thin-lipped smile, as though he knew the secrets of the world. "I saw people buy such things when I was up north. You two will collect herbs. One herb each day. After coriander, you'll bring me caraway, fennel, juniper, mint, onion, poppy, and saffron. And soon, as the weather changes, you'll be able to find garlic." Father rubbed his hands in anticipation. "Think how fragrant fennel bread will be—and onion bread, ah! Wouldn't you eat them?"

Kepi imagined those smells. They were good in greens and fish. But in bread? She tried to put on a positive face, though. "I would always eat your bread, Father." That was the truth at least; if she didn't eat Father's bread, she wouldn't have bread. "And so will Babu, when he's big enough."

"Silly Kepi. I wouldn't waste bread on a baboon. He

already costs us too much to feed. That's why I want him helping you gather herbs. If he's going to live with us, even briefly, he has to do his share."

Even briefly? What did that mean? Kepi brought a lock of her hair to her mouth and sucked on the tips.

"He can climb to places you can't reach and pick any plants you point out to him. We'll make bread as fancy as the pharaoh's. Fancier!"

Kepi looked down.

"Don't let your mother see you doing that." Father brushed the lock of hair from Kepi's mouth. "I can hear your thoughts, you know."

Kepi jerked her head up in surprise. "I thought only the gods could hear thoughts."

"It's a trick of fathers with their youngest daughters. Don't act stubborn, Kepi. Go collect herbs. No one will be able to resist my breads. When old Ashai heard my plans, he made me promise him ten loaves a day for the rest of his life."

"Ten a day for all his life! That's so many."

"Don't be silly, Kepi. His hair is changing color. He must be forty already. He won't last much longer. That's what makes it good business. Listen to this: He said if he likes the bread, really likes it, in exchange he'll give us his wheat field closest to ours."

"Really?"

"Three days ago I hired men to plow it with wooden axes. They're sowing today. We'll have more wheat than ever, for more bread than ever. Bread is as good as pharaohs' gold, my daughter. We'll be rich, even with this lame foot. And I'll get rid of our outdoor latrine."

Kepi gaped. "Don't rich people have needs like ordinary people?"

Father laughed. "Of course they do. But rich people have rooms inside their homes for that. I saw them up north. Copper tubes under the ground carry everything to the river. Go now, Kepi. Don't come home till the basket brims with coriander."

Kepi ran inside for the basket, jangling all the way. Mother and Nanu sat on a small carpet side by side stitching, caressed by sweet coils of fragrance from the incense stick. It had been months since anyone had taken the time to repair clothes, much less make new ones. But that cloth certainly looked like something new. "Is that a dress for you?" Kepi peeked around her sister's side. "The shoulder straps are thin. You'll look all grown up."

Nanu tossed her hair. "I am all grown up."

"Ah. Well then, I suppose you wouldn't care where I'm going. You used to think it was fun. A few months ago. When you weren't all grown up. But now, well, now you wouldn't care."

"No." Nanu wiggled on her stool. "Probably not."

"I didn't think so. Babu and I will have fun. Without you."

Nanu wiggled more. Finally she turned her head to Kepi. "You little tease. Where are you going?"

"They're sowing the new wheat field today," Kepi crowed triumphantly.

"We have a new wheat field?" Nanu looked at Mother. "Please can I go?"

"We don't have a new wheat field." Mother gathered the dress into her lap and folded it. "Your father has ideas. Grandiose plans." She sounded scornful. "If they work out, our fortunes will change. If they don't, he will have spent a lot of money on someone else's field. Money we can't afford to lose. We'll be ruined even faster. Those plants had better grow in record time." She put her palm over her mouth for a moment. "Go if you want. Be part of your father's dream. But don't let Kepi's silliness keep you long. We have work to do." She held out her hand, palm up. "Kepi, leave me your jewelry."

"But I'm not going out to work in the fields, I'm just . . ."

"Careless. You lose everything."

"I used to be that way. But I'm not anymore."

"Since when?" said Nanu. "Yesterday?"

Kepi made a monster face at Nanu.

"Let's be cautious and save ourselves trouble," said Mother.

Kepi put her bracelets and anklets and neck amulet in Mother's hands. She grabbed the basket with one hand and Nanu with the other. The girls ran out the door toward the new wheat field. Nanu's bracelets tinkled the whole way. But that was all right. Kepi would do her task and be home by midday and put on all her jewelry again and dance around the house tinkling. Father would be happy soon. Everything would be all right.

4
FIGS

When Kepi and Nanu got to the field, they watched men in loincloths scatter seeds from cloth bags strung around their necks. The men sang as they worked. Kepi sang, too. She loved the fieldworkers' songs. Babu wiggled around on her head happily. He always did a wiggle dance when Kepi made music, no matter what kind.

The workers must have started at dawn, because they were almost at the end of the field already. They finished and waved to a group of small boys waiting by the side. The boys ran off.

"Are you watching, little Babu?" Kepi reached up and played with the fingers of the baboon on her head.

Nanu gave a playful yank to Babu's foot, and her bracelets jangled sharply. "The best part is about to start."

Minutes later the boys returned, driving a herd of goats. The goats butted and chased one another all over the field, trampling the seeds down into the dirt through their play. The boys had to swat any that tried to eat the seeds. But that didn't seem to dismay them. They frolicked. They were so funny, Kepi found herself dancing. "The birds won't get a quick meal off this field. Father's plan will work."

"You know about his plans?" Nanu's beautiful pink mouth hung open. "How come everyone knows but me? What's going on?"

"Father's going to have the best bakery ever. He'll get famous. And we'll get rich."

Nanu bit her bottom lip and smiled. "And I . . . ?"

"Can get married."

"So how will he make his bakery the best?"

"This basket is part of it all. Babu and I are going to gather coriander to flavor the bread."

"Coriander? That would make awful bread."

"That's what rich folk up north eat."

Nanu frowned. "No one here will want it."

"Yes, they will. And, anyway, he won't make only coriander. He'll make poppy and caraway and . . ."

Suddenly Nanu laughed. "I get it! You're making that up, aren't you? Little liar. That's the worst idea I ever heard."

"It's the truth. Babu and I are going to fill this basket."

"Pah! Well, whatever you're really planning on doing,

hurry and do it. I'm going home to finish my dress." She gave a sly smile. "Someone might want to see me in it."

Did Nanu have her eye on a boy already? But Nanu would never tell her. So Kepi decided not to give her sister the satisfaction of asking.

"Coriander . . ." Nanu shook her head and gave a little wave. "Bye, silly."

Kepi watched Nanu walk away. That was the third time this morning that Kepi had been called silly. Twice by Father, and now Nanu. They always called her that. But right now it shook her, because it wasn't Kepi's idea that Nanu found silly. It was Father's. And everything depended on it. Like Mother said, if it didn't work, they'd be ruined.

All those herbs Father had named . . . none sounded good. Maybe herb bread was a bad idea. Maybe Father's liver was sick and he couldn't think right. Maybe everyone would react like Nanu. And of course they would. Kepi had.

This was terrible. Kepi had to think of a way to fix things. Father wanted to make special bread so he could get more and more customers. What would make bread special? What did Kepi most love to eat?

Fruits. Why not? Fruits were sweet, so fruit breads would be wonderful. Only nothing was in season yet. Mulberry and elderberry would be soon. And dates after that. But Father had spent a lot of money on having the new field sowed, all because he thought he'd be selling everyone bread right away. So Kepi needed fruit today.

And now a wonderful plan came to Kepi. Figs at the very tops of the trees must get missed in the harvest. Some of them, at least. Babu could climb up and throw them down to her. They'd be dried out. But Kepi had seen Mother boil dried fruit, then squash it and use the juices to flavor food. They could do that with old figs, easy. And figgy bread would be purple! Everyone would want it. Father could make beautiful, sweet fruity breads instead of ugly, yucky herb breads.

Kepi marched off toward the fig grove full of hope. But pitiful few figs still clung to the treetops. And those that the baboon threw down had been ravaged by birds and snakes. These figs were far too sweet to go undiscovered by animals.

But, oh, sycamore trees had figs, too—inferior ones not nearly so sweet as grove figs. And those figs grew in the wild, so many trees went unharvested. The animals couldn't have gotten all of them. Ripe wild figs were red inside, not purple. But red would be a wonderful color for bread, too. Kepi laughed. Who wouldn't want red bread?

Tall sycamores were easy to spot, since they grew near the river, where the view was clear. Kepi walked directly to the riverbank and turned north to walk with the current. It wasn't long before she saw a huge spreading tree. The lower branches had been picked clean by gazelles. And the midlevel ones were close to bare, too, being at the right height for the rare giraffe. But higher up many old, withered fruits still dangled. Kepi didn't like heights. One fig, though, hung lower than the others. She put the basket on the ground, climbed, and picked it, then climbed back down.

She lifted Babu off her head and placed him on the ground. Then she dropped the fig into the basket. "See, Babu? You do it now." She pointed at the figs high up. Babu scampered up the tree. He threw down a fig, straight into the basket. Babu really was the smartest little baboon in the whole wide world. Kepi clapped. "Do it again."

Kepi watched the figs plop one by one into the basket. Until something else came hurtling down. Round and plump. Kepi picked it up. It was hard outside.

With a sharp stick, she slit it open. The inside looked like a cluster of tiny flowers meeting head-to-head in the center. White wormy things moved among them. Instantly Kepi recognized them: wasp larvae. Wasps were important to the tree—anyone knew that. Without them, the tree couldn't fruit. Kepi shouldn't have opened this ball. She had to close it up and secure it shut with a leaf and then jam the whole thing someplace safe so the larvae could grow into wasps.

A couple of the larvae had wiggled free and fallen to the ground. So the first job was to rescue them. Kepi picked one up carefully and poked it back into the shell. "Aiii!" Her finger was on fire. And there, emerging from the tiny flowers slowly and jerkily, was a giant wasp. Kepi had been unlucky enough to slit open the very shell where the queen was hibernating. She needed to plunge her hand into the cool river.

She turned toward the water, and a boy was running right at her. He was slight and probably not even her age. But the fierce look in his eyes made her heart jump.

Kepi spun and fled. The boy's feet thumped behind her. His breath came in loud pants. He caught her by the elbow and yanked her back the other way. She screamed and beat her fists on him. He put his hands up in front of his chest defensively and muttered something incomprehensible as he backed off.

Kepi had time to catch her breath. The boy's head was shaved except for a lock at the side, like any child, but he wore no eye makeup, and his loincloth was leather, not linen. He wasn't Egyptian. With his thick neck and high cheekbones, he was surely Nubian. Why would he chase her like that?

Babu came running on all fours through the grasses,

pounced onto the boy's head from behind, and bit one of his small ears, then quickly leaped onto Kepi's head.

The boy cupped his ear and moaned loudly.

Kepi felt suddenly confident. "That's what you get for chasing me. And this is what you get for yanking me." She kicked him. A Nubian might not understand her words, but anyone understood a kick.

The boy hopped, clutching his bruised shin and moaning even louder. And to think that she'd been afraid of him.

A shout came. Kepi now saw a second boy; he waited on the shore, holding a rope attached to a small boat. He was older and stronger. Blue marks ran up both sides of his abdomen. And his face looked mean. Two against one. Kepi's insides went cold. There was a broken branch on the ground not far off. She backed slowly toward it.

The younger boy stopped hopping. He shouted something back to the boat boy, who shouted a long string of gobbledygook. The boy untied the sides of his loincloth with both hands at once and ran at Kepi. She lunged for the stick, but the boy threw the square of leather over her head. The next thing she knew, a powerful blow to the belly knocked her to the ground. The back of her head hit with a *thunk*. For an instant she couldn't hear anything at all. Then she felt her hair being pulled so hard, she thought her scalp was ripping. She pushed up onto her elbows and blinked till her eyes focused again. The boy was running to the boat with a wriggling roll of leather under his arm. A skinny black tail trailed from it, flicking wildly.

5

RUNNING

"Stop!" Kepi ran to the riverbank and shook the stick at them. "Stop, thieves! Stop!"

The current carried the little boat quickly to the center of the river. The bigger boy steered with a paddle while the younger one fiddled with Babu—tying him tight.

"That baboon is Tehuti in disguise!" Kepi shouted. "You're cursed!" That was a downright lie, but Kepi was desperate. Father told a story in which the god Tehuti disguised himself as a baboon and went into Nubia. If these two boys really were Nubian, and if they knew the tale and recognized Tehuti's name, maybe they'd be so frightened, they'd let Babu go. "Tehuti!" she shouted. "Tehuti! Tehuti! Tehuti!"

Both boys paddled vigorously now.

Kepi ran and ran. The back of her head ached where it had smacked the ground. Her stung finger throbbed. But she ran hard. A fast person could outrun a boat, and Kepi was fast.

Those boys didn't scare her. Kepi was sure the littler one had head butted her; he'd never have been strong enough to slam her to the ground like that with just his fists. And while the big one looked strong, he might be a coward. After all, he'd stayed at the boat and left all the dirty work to the littler one. Kepi would throttle both boys good if she could only get to them. But the water was deep, and Kepi wasn't a good swimmer like Nanu was. Besides, the water hid crocodiles, and even though it was still only midday, if a girl happened to step on his back, a hungry crocodile might not wait till dinnertime.

Well, she'd just have to outwit the boys. They would come to shore sooner or later—and as long as it was on her side of the river, she could catch them.

She ducked behind plants as she ran so the boys wouldn't see her if they looked. This section of the flood-plain was cultivated with barley, wheat, and flax pretty much continually all the way to the big city of Wetjeset-Hor. The ground was soft and her feet were strong. She could do this.

Now and then the little boat disappeared from sight, and Kepi had to run harder until it was in sight again. The sun wasn't that hot, but she was moving so fast, she worked up a lather. Sweat drops burned her eyes.

How could they go that fast? The boat was made
of bundled reeds lashed together and curved upward at
both ends—like the kind Egyptians used, but even more
narrow and not quite so long. A boat that shape would
certainly travel the rapids better. But the boat seemed to
travel the open river better, too. It skimmed along northward as though it was going with the wind instead of
against it. She was falling farther and farther behind.

There was only one chance—if the boys were stopping at Wetjeset-Hor, she might be able to get them.

The fields stopped abruptly, and Kepi found herself in an open area that held circular stone structures
arranged around large boulders. There was a place
like this near where Kepi lived, so she recognized
what it was: a small cemetery—the kind from long
ago. The boulders were natural to the earth, but the
circular stones marked graves. Kepi pressed her lips
together hard to keep from shuddering. Who knew
what was under the ground? Father said that long
ago they put bodies right in the earth, without coffins
or even reed mats wrapped around them. Sometimes
the floods would loosen them, and when the waters
receded, bones would litter the area.

Kepi sucked on a lock of her hair and straightened
up to full height. She walked tall like that, eyes on the
ground, and picked her way carefully, to show her respect

for the dead. She wouldn't tread on a single bone.

Once she had passed the last grave marker, she looked ahead on the river. The little boat was out of sight! She barreled through thickets, paying no attention to the thorns that scratched at her arms.

A loud hiss stopped her. A huge ibis stood right in Kepi's path, not two body lengths away. She stared; from the bird's long, curved beak hung a glistening white rope. The ibis fanned out his tail, stretched his curvy neck long and straight, and erected his crest. Specks of blood sparkled on his black feet. Oh! That rope was an animal's nerve. A big animal.

"Hello, ibis," said Kepi in a friendly voice, though she couldn't hold back her tremble. After all, it was a crime to disturb an ibis. They protected the crops and ate the eggs of crocodiles. "Please, let me pass. Thieves took my baboon, and I have to hurry."

The bird gave a cackling cry: *Te-hu te-hu te-hu te-hu!*

"Tehuti?" breathed Kepi. In Father's stories the god Tehuti came not just in the form of a baboon, but also in the form of an ibis. But this couldn't be the god Tehuti in disguise. It couldn't. The gods never showed themselves to Kepi.

Kepi gave the bird wide berth as she walked. The bird just watched her. Once she was past, she whispered, "Thank you." She wanted to move quickly again now.

But the thickets seemed to grow ever more dense. She pushed her way through until she suddenly burst out on the other side.

It was as though she had entered a different world. A giant pile of rot spread before her. The stench was so unexpected, she gagged. Two more ibises poked around in the carcass of an ox. That's where the nerve must have come from. The ox clearly hadn't been killed for food, since his whole body had been left. What a waste. Kepi had never tasted ox; it was far too expensive a meat. Her family ate goat on holidays, but fish the rest of the time. This ox had died recently; it was in better shape than the other carcasses. The remains right beside it she recognized as a ram only with difficulty. This was a dump for animal bodies. Crows hopped through, stealing from one another.

A hand stuck out from under a clutter of feathers and tails. It was curled up and dried out, but a human hand for sure.

Kepi clutched her stomach and doubled over till she was in a squat. Her village had a refuse pile at the outskirts. Every village did. But human remains were never in them. That poor person, disposed of like trash. No one could come visit his grave; he'd die the second death, the death of being forgotten. Kepi rocked on her heels.

When she finally dared to look around again, her eyes met those of a cat sitting on the other side of the ram carcass. Its eyes turned away, and it pounced. Kepi heard a death screech. The crows screamed and took to the air. The cat trotted off with a rat caught in its jaws. The crows quickly settled back down to their squabbling.

A vulture wheeled overhead. Two black kites glided high above him. The tips of their wings spread like greedy fingers. How could the sky look so clean and fresh, all clear blue and white, when the earth below it was a slime of blood and gore?

Te-hu te-hu te-hu! The giant ibis now pushed through the bushes and stepped into the pile of rot. He eyed Kepi.

Kepi gulped. The bird looked like he was going to chase her. That snapped her to attention. The city of Wetjeset-Hor had to be close. If only the boys had stopped there . . . She stood and picked her way carefully past the refuse pile, then broke into a run.

The mud-brick buildings of the town appeared immediately. Kepi stayed near the water, but she couldn't keep herself from glancing up the narrow streets, so full of people and carts and geese and goats and sheep. She came to the city only for special occasions, and never alone. It would have been a thrill to stop and gape, if only this wasn't such an urgent mission. Maybe once

she got Babu, they could take a little while to marvel at
the variety of pots and cloths and hides and jewelry and
foods—at all of it, before starting home again. Father
and Mother couldn't fault her for that.

A string of fishing boats was docked along the river,
their harpoons cleaned and drying in the sun. And trade
boats, too. There were so many in so many sizes. Kepi
inspected them as she wove her way among men in noisy
conversation.

And there was the little reed boat, bobbing between
two fishing boats. Kepi crept closer. The younger boy
was nowhere to be seen, but the older boy lay in the
bottom of the boat, on his back with his eyes closed. A
small handheld drum lay beside his head. His left hand
rested on his chest; his right hand was hidden from her
sight. The blue marks on his abdomen showed clearly
now—two parallel patterns of slash marks, as though
ticking off years. Or conquests. Something about this
boy's posture—maybe just the length of him, maybe the
definition of his arm and leg muscles, maybe all of it
together—gave Kepi the sense that he was exceptionally
strong. Her skin turned to gooseflesh.

Along the side of the boy closest to Kepi was a cloth
covering various lumps. Kepi watched, hoping the cloth
would move. She dared another step closer.

The boy's eyes opened. There had been no special noise to wake him—it just happened. He squinted against the sun and pushed himself up and finally saw Kepi. Instantly his right hand appeared, with a knife!

6
MENES

Kepi turned and ran up an alley. She didn't dare look back for fear of losing time if the Nubian boy was at her heels, knife in hand. She ran past shops with their wares hanging outside, merchants calling out the virtues of their goods. All so much chaos. It made her feel confused and lost and even more frightened. She turned a corner and ran to the next corner and turned again.

Finally, a quiet street. She stopped and swallowed. Then she peeked back into the last street. There was no sign of the boat boy. She leaned her back against a wall and waited for her heart to stop pounding.

Everything had gone wrong. Kepi had planned to simply catch up with the boys and shame them, maybe in public if that's what it took, maybe even with another kick or two, and get her Babu back. Instead, she'd passed a deserted cemetery, she'd seen a human hand under animal carcasses, and that boy's knife was big and sharp. A spasm shot up her back at the memory. A knife like that could kill in a second.

If Kepi died here in Wetjeset-Hor, she'd be a stranger. Unclaimed. They might throw her body in the dump beside the ox. Why, if Kepi persisted in this chase, she could become ibis flesh. Or worse, rat flesh. Without a grave, no one could visit her. A part of a human always lingered at the grave—the *ka*. No one would come to make offerings to Kepi's *ka*. No one would recite magic words over her bones. Her *ka* would be abandoned, all alone into eternity. Kepi's mouth hung open at the thought of such a hideous fate.

She could hear her sister Nanu in her heart. She could hear Mother and Father. All of them were calling her names. Not silly—no, they were calling her crazy. Kepi had been crazy to come this far after two Nubian boys. She couldn't get Babu back. The knife left no doubt.

Tears came in a gush.

When they finally stopped, Kepi wiped her face with the hem of her dress. She should start home. Fast. And when she got near her village, she had better find that sycamore fig tree and retrieve the basket. Father was going to be angry enough at her without her having lost the basket, too. And tomorrow she'd go collect sycamore figs. Tomorrow she'd talk Father into making fruit breads. Tomorrow she'd turn everything right again.

She just had to get home first. That was all.

But she didn't dare walk the path she had come, past the refuse pile. It would turn dark soon, and jackals and hyenas were bound to feast there. Plus crocodiles would wake and wait, their stomachs empty, the whole length of the riverbank.

"Hey, girl, is something wrong?" A tall ropy-looking man stood in the doorway of the building across the alley from her. The odor coming out the door told her it was a brewery.

Kepi shook her head.

The man walked till he was directly opposite her; then he leaned against the wall and crossed his legs at the ankle and studied her. "You look like you've just had bad news." He took the end of a loaf of bread out of a cloth bag and ripped it in half and held a piece out to her. "Hungry?"

It wasn't near dinnertime yet. But all that running had made Kepi hungry. It would be a long time before she got home. And the bread looked good. Still, she didn't know this man. She shook her head.

The man smiled and took a big bite of bread. "I don't live here. Do you?"

Kepi shook her head.

"I didn't think so. Looking as sad as you do, I figure you'd run home if home was nearby. Come on, don't be stubborn. Have some bread. It'll cheer you up." He held out the unbitten half of the bread again.

Father had told Kepi not to be stubborn just this morning. It felt good to have this stranger say it, too, as though this were a normal moment and not the awful one it truly was. And his *shenti*—the cloth that wound around him and covered him from waist to knee—was nice and clean; he looked like a well-mannered man. Kepi crossed the alley and reached for the bread. She took a bite. "It has honey in it," she said. And she burst out crying again.

The man tilted his head. "Honey makes you cry?"

"Honey makes me think of little Babu. He loves honey. And he's gone."

"I'm sorry," said the man gently. "Was he your baby brother?"

"He's my baby baboon."

The man blinked and stood up straight. "You have a baby baboon?"

"Not anymore. Two boys stole him."

"Here in town?"

"No. Babu and I were gathering sycamore figs. He's the smartest baboon in the world. He does anything I tell him. And those boys saw us—the tree was near the river and they were in a boat, and they stole him. He bit one of them really hard, too—but they stole him anyway. I followed them all the way here."

The man furrowed his brow. "How did a girl like you get a baboon?"

"A crocodile ate his mother."

The man opened his mouth as if to ask a question, then shut it. He pulled on the tips of his beard. "So where are the boys now?"

"Their boat is docked with the fishing boats."

"Is there anything special about the boat?"

"What do you mean?"

"How could I recognize it?"

"It's an ordinary boat—just small. But the boys are easy to recognize. They're the only Nubians I saw at the docks."

The man looked hard at Kepi. "Is everything you're telling me the truth?"

She nodded.

"Everything?"

She nodded.

The man pursed his lips. "Where do you live?"

"In a village south of here."

"All right. I have an idea. I think I can help you get your baboon back. Come with me."

7

THE BASKET

"Well, don't just stand there." The man named Menes beckoned to Kepi. "Climb on board."

Kepi's fingers clutched the sides of her skirt nervously. It was one thing to walk with this man through the city streets, where if she screamed someone would come to her rescue. It was quite another to get on a boat with him. She took a step backward.

"You pick now to stop trusting me?" Menes stood in the middle of the boat and stroked his beard. "You remind me of my little sister, you know that? Do you have a sister?"

Kepi nodded.

"They're a raging trouble, right?" He rolled his eyes.

Kepi smiled. "Nanu can be a raging trouble."

"Nanu? That's my sister's name, too!"

Kepi couldn't help smiling. "How funny!"

"Well, from a brother of a raging-trouble Nanu to a sister of a raging-trouble Nanu, if you want to understand my plan, you have to take a look." Menes walked to a cluster of five large baskets and held up the lid of one. He pointed inside.

Kepi sucked on the tip of a lock of her hair.

Menes shrugged. "Look, Kepi, what's the worst that could happen? We're on the dock of a city. It's a busy place. If you shout, someone's going to come running."

The boat was a big one, for cargo. It was made of planks woven together with reeds. Wooden slats fitted into slots between the planks, and more reeds were packed in to seal the seams. Rush matting ran down the center. Five oars lined each side, and two more stuck out of the broad overhanging stern for steering. It had a tall mast for the sail, which was lowered now. There would be a big crew on a boat like this. Maybe twelve men. Maybe more. The more people there were, the less dangerous it was. And, like Menes said, there were other people coming and going on the docks as they spoke. If she shouted, someone would help.

Besides, they had something in common—raging-trouble sisters named Nanu.

And most of all, Menes was nice. He was offering to help her when no one else was. She was lucky he'd come along just at that moment, just when she had decided to go home—without Babu. Kepi had lost so many things in her life, but losing Babu would be the worst by far.

Kepi took a deep breath and carefully walked the little plank and stepped onto the boat. She was surprised to find that the boat didn't move at all with her weight. It was much more stable than the only other boat she'd ever been in—the little one that carried her family to the city a couple of times a year.

Menes smiled at her and backed away to let her pass. Kepi peeked inside the coiled basket. It was empty and smelled of nothing other than the dried bundles of date palm leaves that it was made of. "You sell baskets?"

"Nah. We buy stuff and fill them as we go."

"All right, an empty basket." She shrugged. "What's your plan, anyway?"

"You hide in the basket. I'll go get Babu from the Nubian boys, bring him back here, and put him in the basket with you."

Kepi crossed her arms. She'd been half expecting Menes to offer precisely that, because he'd asked her so many questions about the baboon. But a cold cube of fear formed in the center of her chest. "Why do we have to hide in the basket?"

"If my fellow crew members see you before we leave, they won't let you stay on board. We don't pick up passengers. It's a rule."

"I don't want to stay on board anyway."

"Sure you do. You told me how long it took you to run here. You can't possibly get back home before night-fall—and it isn't safe for you in the dark. So you need a ride with us."

"You're going south?"

"All the way to Yebu."

Yebu was an island in the Nile right on the border with Nubia. The southernmost city of Egypt was there. So this boat would definitely pass by Kepi's village. "But once you leave the dock and I come out of the basket, what's to stop the crew from putting me off onto the shore?"

"By then you'll practically be home already. We'll just explain. No one would ditch a little girl on the shore in the dark. Really. My fellow crew members aren't bad men. They just don't want to break the rules."

Kepi looked into the basket again. It was roomy. Cavernous, in fact. She was sure she could lie down flat in it without her feet or head touching the sides. "How will you get Babu?"

"Leave that up to me. You said he likes goat milk, right?"

"With honey mixed in. He sucks it from my fingers."

"I'll bring him back, and I'll bring dinner for both

of you. So . . . what will it be? Should I lift you in or not?"

"I have to take care of my needs first."

"Go off the side of the boat. I'll look the other way."

Kepi hopped from foot to foot. Now that she'd admitted her need, she could hardly hold it off. "What if someone on the dock sees? And I could fall in. I have to go find a latrine in the city."

"No, you don't. Look." Menes dug through a pile of gear at the bow of the boat. "Here. Get behind the basket and go in this bowl, then dump it over the side."

So Kepi did what she had to. "What should I do with the bowl?"

"Put it back where it came from."

"But it's all nasty now."

"We're used to nasty."

What if that meant the bowl had been used by others, too, without being cleaned out? Kepi held the bowl as far from her as she could and quickly put it back near the pile of gear.

Menes stood beside the basket with his fists on his hips. "Are you finally ready for me to lift you in?"

There was a line of barrels nearby, on the other side of a loop of rope as thick as her waist. Kepi tipped a barrel and rolled it on its bottom rim, just as she rolled the grain barrel at home. She climbed on it, then jumped into the basket on her own. When she stood, only her head stuck out.

Menes smiled. "You look like a funny little monkey yourself. Tell me something. When the croc ate Babu's mother, were there any other baboons around?"

"There had been. But they left."

"Did you see the adult males?"

"There was only one. It was a small band."

"What did he look like?"

"Big, with a lot of silver hair fluffing out around his neck, and a pink bottom."

Menes slapped himself on the chest and let out a loud breath. "A hamadryas. The best kind. Those males are ferocious unless you tame them as babies. Well, I'd better go fetch that baby." He dug into his cloth bag and pulled out a little pouch. "Chew on these while I'm gone."

Kepi took the pouch. "What is it?"

"Something to calm you. Just chew on them." He picked the lid up off the ground. "Sit down so I can close you in."

"What if I want to get out?"

"Stand up and open the lid and shout. But really, don't do that. I mean it. If anyone sees you, the whole plan will be ruined. I'll be back soon. Eat those seeds and wait for me."

Kepi squatted, and the lid closed over her. All light was shut out. Immediately she stood up and lifted the lid.

Menes stood there. He grinned as though that was exactly what he had expected her to do. He mimicked picking things from his hand and eating them. "The pouch," he said. Then he waved good-bye.

She settled back down, this time on her bottom. She couldn't hear much from inside the basket, the coils were stitched together so tightly. She couldn't hear Menes's feet go down the plank.

Would he really get Babu? How long would it take? Kepi chewed on her hair in the pitch dark. Then she remembered Father stopping her from doing that this morning. It seemed like forever ago. By now Father would have realized she wasn't coming home with a basketful of coriander, but he'd be too worried to be angry. Mother and Nanu would be worried about her, too, just as worried as she was about Babu. If only there was a way to let them know she was fine.

She had the urge to get out of this basket. She didn't have to call for help. She could just throw her weight against the side and tip it over. Then she could run after Menes and get Babu back with him. Only Menes had said he didn't want her anywhere near the Nubian boy's knife. And Kepi didn't want to be anywhere near that knife either.

She stood and lifted the lid just a little. She peeked out. Two men on the dock were busy talking. They were easily within shouting distance. Menes was right; this dock was a busy place. Kepi closed the lid and sat.

8

POPPY SEEDPODS

Kepi had never been good at waiting. And this time was harder, because she knew she should be on her way home rather than sitting in the basket. Now that she'd figured out how to make Father's bread famous, she wanted to tell him fast, before he made coriander bread and lost all his customers.

But she also wanted to get Babu back. It couldn't take Menes that long, could it?

The pouch Menes had given her sat on her lap. She opened it and let her fingers investigate. There were three egg-shaped, pliable things, with a little circle of fringe at one end. Seedpods. She held one to her nose. The delicate, pleasant odor of poppy reassured her. Mother ate poppy when she had headaches or trouble sleeping. Lots of people did. And everyone gave teething babies poppy to chew on. So Menes must be right; poppy must be soothing.

Kepi slit the side of one pod with her thumbnail and

sucked out the milky liquid. Then she dug off a small piece of the fibers and put it in her mouth. Her tongue located a few tiny hard balls. She picked the fibers from her mouth but rolled the seeds around on her tongue a minute. Then she used her tongue to push them between her teeth, and she chewed slowly. When she finished, she did the same to another piece, until she had used up one whole seedpod that way.

Everything seemed to slow down. Slow slow slow. Warmth crept through her toes and fingers, up her legs and arms, it seeped through the innards of her body, it leaked in through her ears and nose and eyes. She looked down at where she knew her hands must be and couldn't understand why they didn't glow. She was glowing, she knew she was glowing. If only she had her jewelry on, she could tinkle and glow. Like the goddess Hathor. She giggled.

Ever so slowly she lowered herself backward until she lay on her side, curled gently. This basket was turning out to be a comforting spot to rest. In fact, it was the best place to rest she could ever imagine. How funny. Maybe she could talk Father into trading for a giant basket like this one so that she could nap in it sometimes. Maybe Nanu would nap in the basket with her. And Mother, too. It was big enough for three. Kepi wanted to talk to them about it, describe every detail, so Father could buy another one exactly like this one. This one was the best in the world. It made her feel not only rested but now full of energy. She wanted to stand up and dance. But her arms weren't moving, her legs weren't moving. It was like they weren't hers—they were far too relaxed to move. She'd have to think about that. Later. She smiled into the dark. Later.

A rasping whisper came from above. "Psst! Kepi! Psst!" Kepi sat up. She felt no alarm, just a pleasant dazedness. She looked right at Menes, who smiled down at her. Really? He had left only a second ago. Could he really have come back already? Or maybe she'd slept? But she didn't think she'd slept.

Menes handed her a wiggling cloth bundle, knotted at the top. Kepi breathlessly untied it. Babu jumped on her head and clung there, making little cries like lamb bleats. Kepi squeaked, too. She had never been so happy. She reached up and pulled her dear baby down to her chest and hugged him close, kissing the top of his head. He was really back. It was what she had hoped for, but it felt too good to be true.

She looked up, but Menes's head had disappeared. All she saw was sky. Twinkling sky. So time had passed, after all. Well, that was good. In fact, nothing could be a better omen. Those twinkles were Kepi's ancestors, the imperishable ones, telling her everything was going to be all right. Everything was going to be all right from now until forever. She laughed out loud.

And there was the moon, looking benevolent. Was that really the goddess Hathor? Could it be that for once a goddess cared about her? "I love you," called Kepi. "I love you so much."

"I love you, too." The words rang through the night air clean and clear. "You take care of that baboon now."

Ha!

Menes's face reappeared. "Here." He lowered a cloth satchel into the basket. "There's enough food for both of you in there. I'm going to tie the lid shut now. That way, if anyone moves the basket when we rearrange the cargo, it won't fall off accidentally and expose you. So don't try to lift it off this time, all right? No noises. Just eat and rest. And take good care of that baby baboon. That's the important thing."

Kepi smiled and nodded. "Babu and fruit bread. That's all we need."

"Did you suck on a seedpod?"

Kepi smiled and nodded.

"I thought so. Finish them off. All of them." He closed the lid.

"Menes?" called Kepi.

He opened the lid and leaned in. "What is it?"

She waved good-bye to the goddess Hathor, up there

in the sky. "How did you manage to get him?"

"Does it matter?"

And it didn't. Kepi kissed the top of Babu's head. Everything was going to be all right forever. "Thank you."

The lid shut again.

In the dark Kepi felt her way carefully through the food satchel. She wiggled the stopper free from a jar, and the unmistakable sharp scent of goat milk and honey made her mouth water. Babu cried instantly—the poor hungry little one. He was still used to several meals a day.

Kepi fed him from her fingers. He whimpered between gulps, like a wounded puppy. She fed him till he curled in her lap, asleep. She snaked her hand between his arms and felt his belly. It was a hard, round ball. A happy ball.

She held the jar to her chest. She wanted the rest of that milk; she could almost taste it, she wanted it so bad. But if Babu should wake before they got home, he might need a little more just for comfort. He was still a baby, after all. She carefully replaced the jar stopper.

Another jar held beer. Kepi took a sip. It bubbled more than the beer Father made at home. She drank a little, then put the stopper back in the jar. A hunk of bread and a folded palm leaf still remained in the satchel. She opened the leaf and her finger sank into soft curds— fresh goat cheese. Menes really was a brilliant man.

He was the most brilliant man in the whole world. She smeared the cheese on the bread and ate a big bite. It was fabulous. But she found she wasn't as hungry as she'd thought. She couldn't take a second bite. She wrapped up the cheese and bread again.

She took another seedpod and bit a little hole in the side and sucked as she lay back down and curled around Babu. They'd be home soon. She closed her eyes. She felt so good, so different. She was exhilarated and at the same time lulled into dreaminess by the sweetness of everything.

Vibrations traveled up from the boat floor through the basket. The crew must be moving cargo around, just as Menes had said they would. Kepi braced herself in case someone should lift the basket. She didn't want to be surprised and let out a yelp by accident. But no one touched the basket.

Of course not. Everything was going to be all right forever and ever and ever.

She chewed on the seedpod lazily.

After a while, the basket shook. That must have been from the *thunk* of the stone anchor onto the deck, she thought groggily. So they'd be going now. South, against the current. That meant the crew would raise the sail. She wished she could hear it going up. She wished she could hear it flutter in the breeze that always blew against the

Nile current. She wished she was already home and lying on her reed mat, listening to Nanu breathe beside her in that lovely regular way of sleep, knowing that, if she called out, Mother would come running. If only Menes would take the lid off so she could watch the lights in the sky as they sailed.

But what did that matter? She could hardly hold her eyes open anyway. Besides, even with her eyes shut, she could see the heavenly lights. She shut them. All those shining dots. A comforting warmth gently rolled across her skin everywhere. Everything was exactly how it was supposed to be. Kepi laughed.

9
STUCK

Kepi woke to coal black. She rubbed her eyes. Something warm and rough touched the heel of her left hand. She would have jumped away in alarm, but her head felt heavy, her whole body felt heavy. Solid, lumpy heavy. She pushed up onto her elbows with effort, wobbled a moment, then surrendered herself and fell back down again. Little grunts came. Oh, thank goodness, it was dear Babu. He must have woken her.

And now she remembered where she was. How long had she been here?

Babu ran his fingers along Kepi's lips. He grunted again. He tried to wriggle his hand inside her mouth.

"Funny baby." Kepi found the energy to search around in the dark for the satchel. She was proud of herself for having thought to save the remainder of the honeyed goat milk in case Babu needed it. She took the stopper off the jar and fed the little baboon from her fingers.

He ate and ate and ate. Gradually Kepi realized

something worrisome: This wasn't just a few little suckles. Babu ate the way he did every morning, after a long night.

Kepi's cheeks went slack. Was it morning? It couldn't be. Menes had said they'd take her home. She should have been home long before morning. Something must have changed. Menes's plans had gone wrong. Kepi should get out of the basket. She tried to stand, but it was hard to hold herself up.

She let Babu finish what was in the jar. Then she got to her knees. Babu immediately climbed onto her head. Maybe he could see in the dark? She didn't know. They'd never gone anywhere in the dark before. She got to her feet all crouched over, so she wouldn't mash Babu's head against the lid, and spread her legs in a bracing position, as anyone should on a boat. But she didn't feel the least wobbly. This boat was so big, a person didn't even feel it moving through the water. She reached a hand up to push. The lid didn't budge.

Menes had tied it shut.

He had told her he would. She fought off fear.

A vibration came through the bottom of the basket. Kepi dropped to sitting. She didn't know why she was having so much trouble waking up. She snapped her fingers in front of her face; that's how she usually woke up. Nanu would snap her fingers by Kepi's head, and

Kepi's eyes would fly open and she'd be up just like that. But it didn't work now; she was groggy. She lay back down and stretched out. This basket really was huge. Babu settled on her chest. Her eyes closed on their own. Vibrations came up from the floor.

She rolled in one direction and the side of the basket pushed at her right shoulder. She rolled in another direction. Now it pushed at her feet. She pushed back, only to meet an unyielding force. That was a surprise. When she'd gotten into the basket, nothing had been touching it on the outside.

With both hands, she felt the sides of the basket. Instead of bulging outward in the nice way they had when she first jumped in, they were straight. Her hands moved up and down. Yes, it was as though there were five straight, rigid walls around the basket. Something was pushing against them from the outside.

Kepi pushed back hard now. Nothing happened. She pushed harder. Nothing. She was stuck. Like a wild thing in a cage. Her insides banged around inside the hollow of her body.

She dropped her hands and shouted, "Help!" She shouted until her throat was raw and her ears had gone deaf. Babu whimpered the whole time.

Then came a huge lurch. There was no doubt about it: The boat was moving. And it hadn't been before.

She knew that now for sure.

Nothing was the way it was supposed to be. Panic tightened her skin. Where was Menes? He should know she'd be scared. He should be there, telling her what was going on.

What if Menes wasn't around? What if the boat had left without him and no one even knew she was in this basket?

Kepi tried to dig her fingers between two loops of the basket coil. If she could only make a hole, she could shout through it. She dug. The fibers cut her fingers, but she dug and sucked them and dug some more. Whoever had stitched this basket had done a very fine job.

Kepi searched in the satchel. She found the leaf, opened it, and ate a fingerful of the soft goat cheese. She wasn't hungry, really, but food might wake her up so she could think better. She ate another fingerful. Then she ripped a strip off the date leaf and chewed, sucking the bitter juice. That was when she realized the jar with the honeyed goat milk was empty. So nothing would be lost if she broke it.

She held the jar by the neck and slammed it on the floor. The thick basket bottom cushioned the blow. She tried again and again, but the jar wouldn't break. She tried slamming it against the sides of the basket. But they were just as thick as the bottom. Babu pulled on her hair, his teeth chattering. "Don't worry," she whispered to him. "I'll figure it out." She could bash it against the beer jar, but then they might both break and she'd lose that beer. Anyone who lived near desert knew that losing the only thing you had to drink was too dangerous to risk. She could conk it against her head, but she might knock herself out.

She pulled her dress up to her waist and rearranged herself so she was sitting with one leg straight and one leg bent, knee in the air. She leaned forward and kissed that knee. "I'm sorry," Kepi whispered. "You're a very good knee, but I have no choice. I'm getting really scared. I'm sorry." She brought the jar down as hard as she could on her knee. The blow stunned her, it hurt so bad. Hot blood rolled down her leg in both directions. The jar had broken. The smell of blood sweetened the air.

She gritted her teeth and blinked back tears, then gathered the pottery pieces into a pile near one side of the basket. She moved as little as possible, both because her knee burned and because she was afraid of getting cut on whatever little shards she might have missed. With the biggest shard, she attacked the side of the basket at her shoulder level sitting down. She stabbed and sawed. She couldn't believe how tough the basket was. Sweat covered her and her knee throbbed. She sawed for a long time.

Finally the hole was big enough to stick three fingers through. That would do. She put her mouth to it and shouted. "Help! Help, help, help!"

10
AWAY

Within moments she heard a scraping noise, and the side of the basket went pliable again. Then— "Stop that!" came the hiss. Whoever it was, he must have been squatting, because his mouth was lowered to the hole.

"Let me out!"

"Not yet, Kepi." It was Menes.

"Let me out now!"

"In a while."

"Now! I'm bleeding."

"What? What happened?"

"A jar broke."

"Is the baboon all right?"

Kepi's eyes burned. Her head felt heavy. But the question still seemed suspect. "I'm not sure," she lied. "Let us out."

Menes cursed. The top of the basket shook a little, and soon the lid lifted off and light flooded in.

Kepi blinked against the sun and got to her feet. She let out a yelp because straightening her knee hurt so bad. She stood on her good leg and let her hurt one hang. "Help!" she shouted. "Get me out of here!"

Men sat on the benches along both sides of the boat, rowing. They heard her for sure, but they did nothing. They were facing the stern and her basket was near the stern, so they could easily have looked at her. But only a few even glanced her way, and none stopped rowing.

"Don't waste your breath," said Menes.

Kepi felt tears coming. Why was Menes acting like this? She blinked hard.

"And don't go crying."

"I'm not! I'm blinking because of the sun. It's morning."

Babu climbed up Kepi's back and perched on her head.

"That baboon's all right," said Menes. "You lied."

"The sail's not up." Kepi shook her head slowly in horror as the meaning of that sank in. "We're going with the current. We're going north. Away from my home!"

"Be quiet. I'll explain."

"You said you'd take me home. You said we'd go last night!"

"Boats can't go at night on this river. You saw what the croc did to your baboon's mother. What do you think crocs would do to a boat at night? Don't talk like an idiot."

"I'm not an idiot!" Menes had told her the boat would travel at night, and now he was calling her names for believing him. "No crocodile could turn over this boat."

"But they can ram it hard enough to do damage."

Kepi wanted to punch Menes's smug face. "Where are we going?"

"I'll tell you later."

"Let me out."

"You're better off in the basket."

"I want to go home. Let me out right now."

"If you stay quiet, I'll leave the lid off."

"I'm bleeding."

"I don't believe you."

Kepi reached down and wiped at the wetness above her knee. She thrust a bloody hand in Menes's face.

He blanched. He went over to a box and came back with a cloth. "Tie this around so it covers the cut. Tie it as tight as you can bear."

Kepi snatched the cloth. "Help!" she shouted. "Help!"

One of the men looked at her and smirked. The top half of his left ear was missing. "Hurry up," he called to Menes. "It's hard to keep the boat straight without you at your oar!"

"See? I have to go back to work. I can't be bothered with you now. If you keep shouting, I'm tying the lid back on. And the poppy has clearly worn off, so it will be awful."

"What are you talking about?"

"What do you think poppy seeds do, little idiot? You think you had all those nice dreams all on your own? That's a poppy-seed haze."

Menes had drugged her. Kepi gritted her teeth. "I'm standing. If you push that lid down on me, you'll crush Babu."

Menes frowned.

"Ha! I knew it. You're as bad as those Nubian boys. You want to steal Babu." It was only as she said it that she realized it was true.

Menes grabbed at Babu, but Babu bit his hand. He let out a little shriek and shook his hand and blew on it. "All right, all right. Stand there and yell till you drop, if you're that much of an idiot."

"I'm not an idiot."

"Prove it. Shut your mouth, and I promise, when we stop for a break, I'll explain everything."

"You don't keep your promises."

"Shut your mouth anyway. None of the crew cares

what happens to you. There's no one on the shore to hear you. If we pass a boat going our way, we're obviously going faster than them, so they can't catch us. And if we pass a boat going the opposite way, do you really think they're going to turn around and chase us—a crew this big? Think, Kepi."

Kepi's head spun. No one cared what happened to her? What could that mean? She looked at the men. They were big. She felt small. "Where are you taking me?"

"What did I say? I told you I'd tell you later, right?"

Menes went and got the bowl Kepi had used the night before and offered it to her. She took it numbly.

Menes went back to his oar.

Kepi felt a scream grow inside her chest. It burned her lungs and throat. But if she let it out, Menes would close the basket lid. That would be worse. They were going north, and right now there was nothing Kepi could do about it. She had to think about something else. She'd go crazy if she didn't.

Kepi set the nasty bowl down on the bottom of the basket and inspected her knee. She hadn't dared touch it before, so she didn't know how bad it really was. A piece of the jar still protruded from it. She picked it out, and the bleeding started all over again. She squeezed her eyes shut. The trick here was to pretend this wasn't her knee at all. She was Mother, taking care of her daughter Kepi.

She opened her eyes, and with just the tips of her fingers she gently checked for other pieces. The cut wasn't wide, but it was deep. She carefully placed the cloth on it and tied it behind her knee as tight as she could without wincing. Then she stood on her good leg and looked around.

The boat rode low in the water. The crew had loaded on many smaller baskets since Kepi had come on board. Her basket was surrounded by them; they were what pushed up against the basket sides and made them rigid. She had no idea what was in them.

Kepi looked back. Where were they? She couldn't see any trace of Wetjeset-Hor. It had taken her a while to cut that hole in the basket, so there was no telling how far they were from the city now. The farther they went, the longer it would take her to get home, and her family must already be frantic. They would have searched everywhere for her by now. They probably feared the worst. Kepi feared the worst.

She swallowed hard and willed herself to be strong. Father always said to put a stout heart to a steep hill. She hadn't listened to Father when she'd run off to search for the sycamore figs, and that was when everything had gone wrong. Girls should obey their fathers. She had made a mistake then. But now she'd listen to him. She would remember all his sayings. That way it would be almost as though he was here, whispering to her. He'd be the one person on this boat who cared about her.

On the west bank of the river rose a large red structure, as tall as a sycamore fig. Kepi knew what that was: a pyramid from the old days. Her family had visited it years ago. Though she had been too small then to remember seeing it herself, her parents had talked about it recently, when Father had come home from the north. It was red and rough because in the old days the pharaohs built their pyramids of sandstone instead of limestone. The side of the pyramid ran parallel to the river, so she could see it well, reaching up to a jagged top that the winds and rains had ravaged.

On the east bank a huge rock shaped like a vulture rose up out of the desert. It looked like pictures of the goddess Nekhbet. There were no villages, no isolated farms, no signs of people at all. A cool wind kept the sky clear. Now and then the red sandstone of a hillock would shine, but mostly the banks held widely scattered clumps of low green plants and wading birds, poking their long bills into the mud. This must be how the river valley had looked since the beginning of time.

In late morning a flock of pelicans came flying up the river, straight toward the boat. So many, the flock was as wide as the river. They swerved off to the west and looked like they were going in for a landing somewhere beyond a particularly thick group of bushes. As if that was a signal, the men rowed for shore.

Kepi's stomach pitched with worry. Those bushes probably marked a waterlogged marsh full of crocodiles and hippopotamuses. "Are we stopping?" she called. "Why? Where are we?"

Only Menes looked at her. "Do what I say, and you may just make it out of this."

11
THE LAKE

The crew anchored the boat on the west bank. Since no one was answering Kepi's questions, she kept her mouth shut and watched, trying to notice everything. Father always said details mattered. He said if you focused too much on the snake, you'd miss the scorpion.

Nine men jumped onto the mud, carrying spears and nets. Menes and two other men stayed on board.

Menes came over to Kepi's basket. "Put your arms around my neck and I'll haul you out of there."

"Why? What are we going to do?"

"Stop talking and let me get you out of there."

"If you do anything bad, I'll tell Babu to bite you again. Harder."

Menes glanced quickly at Babu. He licked the raw spot on his hand. Then he looked down at Kepi and lowered his neck.

Kepi locked her arms around Menes's neck and let herself get dragged out. She yelped involuntarily as her injured knee scraped over the basket edge.

Menes set her down and frowned. "Can you walk?"

"I can hop." Kepi hopped. It made her knee hurt worse. She squeezed her eyes shut to keep from tearing up. Then she looked hard at Menes and hopped again.

"Okay, climb on." Menes turned his back to her and squatted. "Come on now. Don't make me wait, or I might change my mind and leave you here."

Kepi thought of the spears the men carried. "How do I know here isn't better than where you'll take me?"

"You don't." Menes shrugged. "But I do. Take this." He held up a cloth satchel. "I'm carrying you—so you carry this for me."

Kepi took the satchel and climbed on, holding her hurt leg out straight. Menes hooked his arms around and under her thighs, careful not to touch the bandage. He lowered himself off the boat.

Two men stayed behind.

"Where are those men going to take the boat?" Kepi asked in sudden panic.

"Nowhere. They're just guarding it. Look around. You'll see beautiful things."

Menes followed the other men's tracks in the mud. Even though he moved slowly, every step hurt Kepi. Plus Babu kept pulling her hair insistently; he was obviously hungry again, and she had nothing for him.

Kepi gritted her teeth and swallowed over and over. She was lost. With poor little Babu to take care of. She wanted Mother. And Father. She even wanted Nanu.

It hurt her knee when she held herself erect, so she slumped against Menes's back and rested her cheek in the little curve where his neck met his torso. Babu chattered in angry discomfort, but Kepi felt too sorry for herself to change positions. Menes's regular loping steps rocked her into a half sleep.

After a while, Menes tapped Kepi on the nose and stopped walking. "Look at that," he whispered.

"Huh?" Kepi lifted her head groggily.

"Don't make noise. Just watch."

They were standing on a small hillock and a lake spread out before them, its perimeter thick with papyrus reeds. Kepi held herself up tall so she could see everything. A herd of oryx grazed in the stubble on the far side, while several of them drank at the water's edge. It wasn't a big herd—maybe a hundred. Their clean black-and-white markings made their faces beautiful. Kepi loved oryx because of those funny faces, though she knew they were dangerous. Their graceful, backward-curving horns were strong enough to kill a lion. Father had told her stories.

But the best thing was the pelicans. The flock she'd watched fly up the river had joined many others. Two islands in the lake were entirely covered with them. Thousands. Gigantic white birds with yellow bills and black-tipped wings. Some were stretching their wings right now and turning in circles on their pale pink legs. The wingspans were enormous, twice a man's height. And there were so many chicks, all gray and fluffy. A small group took off, flying so low, their big bellies almost brushed the water's surface. How wonderful that must feel, flying.

The sun glinted off something in the thickest bushes— a clump of acacia. Kepi watched one of the men with his fist circling the hilt of a knife held ready by his cheek. She spied other crew members now. Three were crawling on their bellies, hidden from the oryx by the reeds. They had spears. They were closing in on a mother and calf. At a flap of the arm from the lead hunter, all three stood and threw spears at the calf. Instantly, other men popped up from behind another group of reeds and shouted and banged metal sticks on a big metal disk. The noise was brash and loud. The herd took off. The poor mother oryx circled her fallen calf once, eyes frantic, then ran with the herd. The air was full of adult pelicans in flight and the screaming cries of their chicks left behind.

The man with the raised knife ran forth from the acacia bushes now and slit the calf's throat. And all the men got busy preparing the meat. They built a fire and wrapped chunks of the meat in wet papyrus to roast in the embers.

Menes carried Kepi down to the lake and deposited her at the very edge of the water. "I'll go get us something to eat."

Strong—stout heart against a steep hill. Kepi looked straight in Menes's eyes. "Babu's hungry, too."

"I didn't bring any more goat milk. It would have rotted in the sun. But there's honey in a jar inside the satchel you're carrying. Wash out your cut and smear some on it, too."

"Honey on a cut? Don't you know anything about wounds? You're supposed to use dung."

"Bathe while you're at it."

"What if there are crocodiles?"

"They'd be pretty dumb pelicans to breed here then, wouldn't they?" Menes walked off.

Kepi looked around. Some of the men were bathing in the lake. It was so shallow, they could stand, even in the middle. Crocodiles preferred deep water, especially in the cooler months, like now. She put her hand in the water. It was cool, but not nearly as chilly as she'd expected. The sun did a better job on shallow pools than on deep ones. Well, all right. She waded in a few steps and sat on the soft silty bottom with all her clothes on. She was old enough to be wary of undressing around men. Besides, this way, she could wash her clothes at the same time.

She rubbed herself all over through her dress. Then she took off the bands that held her locks into pigtails, leaned back, and rinsed out her hair.

Babu screeched in protest and splashed to the shore. He sat there shivering and whimpering in the sunlight.

"Poor Babu," called Kepi, shivering herself. "But I'll feed you now." She hobbled to the shore and shook off. She stayed standing, even though it meant putting all her weight on her one good foot, because that way she'd dry off without getting dirty again. She leaned over and picked up the cloth satchel. Babu climbed up and clung to her chest. "What's the matter? Don't you like wet hair?" Kepi found the jar of honey and fed Babu from her fingers. The little baboon ate eagerly. "Don't get used to it. Honey alone isn't enough for a baboon to grow big on."

Menes came over and spread out papyrus on the ground, with a heap of meat in the center. "You didn't wash out your cut."

Kepi shrugged. The cloth on her knee was soaked through. "I can't undo the knot now that it's wet."

"You should have taken off the cloth before you went in the water."

"Well, I didn't."

"Here." Menes took the honey jar from Kepi and gave her a hunk of meat. Then he took out a knife, knelt, and cut the cloth off her knee. "Impressive gash.

How'd you manage to do that?"

Kepi licked the meat juice from her bottom lip. She had never tasted anything like it. Light and somehow sweet. Very different from goat. "I'm not telling."

"You're a lot of trouble, you know that?" Menes shook his head and grinned up at her. "This looks pretty clean, I guess." He smeared honey on her cut.

"Aiii!"

"It'll help, I swear. And here, eat these." He gave her a handful of freshly pulled wild garlic plants. The bottoms had only barely begun to form bulbs. "They'll make it hurt less."

"I don't believe you."

"Just eat the garlic and try to be reasonable."

Kepi knew it was fine to eat garlic. She washed the plants in the lake and ate slowly. The other men were at the far edge of the lake, lying on the ground near the fire. Some were eating and talking. Some were napping. Only Menes really paid any attention to her.

She was clean; her stomach was full. For a moment, nothing felt threatening. That realization jarred her; she couldn't afford to let her guard down.

12

DECISION

"Why are you stealing Babu and me?"

Menes stretched. "Rescuing, not stealing. You're going to have a much better life this way."

"What are you talking about?"

"I'm taking you to Ineb Hedj."

Kepi's head dropped forward. "That's way up north!"

"At the start of the delta. I'm glad to see you know something, at least."

"Everyone knows about Ineb Hedj. It's the capital of all Egypt."

"It's the biggest city anywhere. And that's where the most important temples are. That's where they use baboons."

Kepi's jaw clenched in fear. "What do mean, use baboons?"

"In the temples. With the *hem-netjer tepey*, the high priest. I bet you've never even seen a priest except at a festival. But I've listened to people talk. It's something new; the rich people all believe in it. Babu will be part of the religious ceremonies. He'll have a wonderful life. And as his trainer, you will, too."

"No. I'm not going to Ineb Hedj. I'm going home. Right now."

"Oh, sure, you're going to limp along the shore, crying from pain, and the very first night a croc will eat you."

Kepi didn't bother to point out that she hadn't cried at all. "I'll walk inland."

"Where a lion will eat you. Listen to me, Kepi. City life is exciting. A lot better than being a country peasant. You've got a chance to change your whole life."

Kepi thought of Nanu and Mother and Father. She thought of the sweet-smelling reed mat she slept on at home and how she always fell asleep watching the lights in the sky out the high window. And most of all, she thought about how much Father needed her right now. "I don't want to change my life."

"You should. Look at you. You're so poor, you don't have a single piece of jewelry. Every Egyptian girl should have at least an amulet. Even a servant. Even a slave. Whoever owns you doesn't deserve you."

"I have plenty of jewelry. My mother made me take it off to go do an errand for my father, because I always lose things."

"You tell too many lies."

"No, I don't. I have a good life. I don't want to change it."

Menes rubbed at the corner of his eye thoughtfully. "All right, then. Go. Go back home. Or go anywhere you want. If that wound doesn't fester, you'll be able to run in another couple of days. Maybe you can make it home alive. I wouldn't bet on it. But who knows. So go. Limp away. Just leave that baboon behind."

"I won't leave Babu."

"And I won't let you take him. So leave—go away on your own. Or come with us. But make up your mind fast, because if you're going to leave, you have to hide somewhere now, while the others are busy. If they know what you're up to, they'll never let you."

Menes didn't know anything about Babu. If Kepi wanted, she could make the little baboon scamper off, out of reach of all the men. They could chase and chase him, but they'd never catch him. Then after they left, she could call to him and they'd be together again: Kepi and Babu.

So losing Babu wasn't really a problem. The problem was everything else.

Kepi looked around. This lake was a safe place—Menes was right. She could stay here till her knee healed. And she could find a sharp rock and cut enough papyrus to make a small boat to carry her and Babu home. Paddling against the current would be hard. So she'd use long sticks as poles, and her dress would make a decent sail stretched between them. They could eat bird eggs, or catch fish, or even eat baby birds if they had to. Babu wouldn't like it, but he'd adjust. Kepi would help him. She'd sing to him; that always made him happy. At night they'd sleep under palm fronds. It would work. Kepi knew survival skills. All those weeks of exploring with Father during the flooding season had prepared her perfectly for this.

Menes thought Kepi couldn't do it. He thought he had her trapped. He knew as little about her as he knew about Babu. She should go hide and let the men leave. Without her.

To Ineb Hedj. The capital.

Pharaoh Khufu lived in the capital.

A small thumping started within her.

Kepi licked her bottom lip. She wasn't an idiot, no matter what Menes said. She didn't fool herself. It would take a while for her knee to heal, and then a really long time to get home in a tiny boat, if in fact she could manage to make a craft that was riverworthy. Days and days. Maybe even weeks. By that time, Father's baking business could have failed completely. He had made a big mistake to pay those men to sow old Ashai's field before he knew whether people liked his herb breads.

Her father didn't really know anything about baking. He was a farmer. He was only doing this because Pharaoh Khufu had sent him home, empty-handed and unable to return to his old work. Pharaoh Khufu had ruined his life.

Someone had to tell the pharaoh what Father was going through. And Father said that another man got hurt in the same accident that he got hurt in. Someone had to tell Pharaoh Khufu to help that man, too. The pharaoh owed it to them.

The thumping inside her grew fast and loud.

Kepi didn't want to go to Ineb Hedj. She didn't like Menes anymore, and she'd never particularly liked the other men. She wanted to go home. That was the right thing for her.

But it wasn't the right thing for her father. Kepi had wanted to fix everything with her idea of fruit bread. That was a bad idea—that made all this trouble. But now she could fix everything a different way.

She'd promised herself that if she ever got the chance to talk to Pharaoh Khufu, she'd take it. What was the point of a promise if you didn't keep it?

"I'll go with you to Ineb Hedj."

Menes had been watching her this whole time. "Good. You're kind of fun." He put the stopper on the honey jar and closed up his cloth parcel. "Eat more. Come on. It's great and you know it."

Kepi forced down a bite. Her body was filled with the drumbeat still, her chest and neck and head were hot, her eyes burned. But this meat was good, and she needed the strength it would give her, and most of all, it was important never to waste meat. Everyone should be grateful for the sacrifice of an animal's life. She silently thanked the oryx calf.

When Menes offered his back to her for the return trip to the boat, Kepi hesitated. She didn't want to act like buddies with Menes. He wasn't her buddy. She was going with him because that was the only way to get to Ineb Hedj. But Menes was the one who had stolen her in the first place. How could she ever understand that? How could she forgive it? She looked around at the other crew members. Wouldn't someone else offer her an arm to lean on? There must be at least one who was halfway nice. But they just walked on by.

Menes finally stood up. "What are you waiting for?" He spit to the side, then wiped his mouth with the back of his hand. "I saw how you looked at the other men just now. Maybe you think someone will help you somehow. No one will. We're all partners. We're going to split the money from trading you."

"Trading me?" Her flesh crawled. "Like a slave? I'm

not a slave. You can't take Egyptian girls and make them slaves. That's against the law!"

"You're Nubian."

"I am not."

"You are if I say you are."

"Then how come I speak Egyptian and I don't understand a word of Nubian?"

"You've been with us long enough to learn Egyptian. And you're just pretending when you act like you don't know Nubian."

"That's not true."

"It is if I say it is." He turned and squatted. "Get on my back."

"I'll walk to the boat on my own."

"You can't. So either get on my back or I'll carry you under my arm and your knee will hurt a lot worse."

"You're awful."

"It's not going to be like a slave, Kepi. You'll have a good life. Really. Especially if they keep you on as the baboon's trainer. Get on. I'll carry you to the basket."

"But I agreed to come. I don't want to stay in the basket like a prisoner."

"It doesn't matter whether you agreed or not. And don't you ever say anything about me offering you a choice. As far as the men are concerned, you're a prisoner. They want you in the basket."

"So I'll tell them I really want to go to Ineb Hedj."

"Who would believe you? They'd figure you just wanted more freedom so you could find a chance to escape." Menes squatted. "Get on."

Kepi held in her fury and climbed onto Menes's back. And the funny thing was, her knee didn't hurt as badly now. Maybe the garlic really did fight pain. Maybe the honey really did help heal. But Menes was awful, all the same. He thought it was all right to steal and trade little girls. She couldn't wait to get to Ineb Hedj so she and Babu could run away from him.

13
THREE IN THE BASKET

Early that afternoon Kepi was standing in her basket on the boat with Babu on her head when they passed shining cliffs on the east bank. Then she saw huge mud-brick walls up ahead on the west bank.

Menes left his bench and came over. He handed her the nasty bowl. "Time to close you in."

"Why?"

"That's the city of Nekhen up ahead. We're stopping there for the night. If you weren't such a problem, you could come out and see things. There are two stone statues of Pharaoh Khasekhemwy. They're over a hundred years old. Big things—life-size. And there's a temple to the god Horus. You couldn't go in it, of course, but it's enough to see just from the outside. And the breweries! They're among the best the entire length of the Nile."

"Babu can't keep eating nothing but honey. He'll get sick. And I'm hungry. You won't be able to sell us if we're sick and hungry. You have to let us out."

"Look out below. The lid's coming down." Menes held the lid high and lowered it fast.

Kepi had barely enough time to crouch out of the way. She quickly pushed up against the lid with both hands. But Menes was obviously pushing back. And soon nothing was pushing back, but the sides of the lid held fast; he'd tied it shut.

She sat on the bottom of the basket. Menes had turned it upside down and dumped all the pottery shards into the river before he put her back in it, so there was no risk of getting cut. The only thing in there with her and Babu was the nasty bowl he had just handed her. Not even the last of the poppy seedpods or the goat cheese was left. Menes must have dumped them in the river, too.

She put her ear to the small hole she had sawed in the side of the basket and listened as the men rowed up to the dock and anchored. She heard them moving about the deck. Then they were gone. Probably not all—probably one or two were still there, guarding whatever was in the baskets. But basically, the crew was off doing whatever the crew did in town, and Kepi was stuck here.

She stretched out in the bottom of the basket, and Babu burrowed under her arm. She was really on a boat, really going to see the pharaoh. All by herself. No mother, no father, no sister. How on earth had her life turned upside down so fast? The magnitude of it hit her. Tears ran hot from the corners of her eyes, down her temples, into her hair. She rocked her head from side to side, on and on and on.

Then she just lay still.

What must Mother be thinking now? And Father, and Nanu? They must be crying. Little girls who disappeared overnight sometimes never came home again. But Kepi would get home again. She wished she could tell them that; she wished she could send a message somehow.

Baaaa! Naaaa!

Kepi's eyes popped open. She must have been in that position for a long time, because her neck had a mean kink. The lid was off the basket, and she looked up straight at the underside of a nanny goat.

"Move," said Menes, outlined by the light from the setting sun.

Kepi stood and hunched against the side. Babu held on to her tight and stared at the goat.

Menes lowered the goat into the basket as far as he could, then dropped her the last little bit. "Fresh milk whenever Babu wants it. What do you think of that?"

"I'm not sharing my basket with a smelly goat."

"When we're docked you are. During the day, when

we're traveling the river, the goat can stay out on deck."

"The goat gets to stay out on deck and I don't?"

"If you prove you're smarter than the goat, I might be able to talk the men into letting you out on deck, too."

"I told you I decided to come with you. I'm not going to escape." At least not till we get to Ineb Hedj, thought Kepi.

"Yeah. Well, the crew sees you as a prisoner. And I'm less than convinced about you." Menes handed Kepi a cloth satchel. "Open the leaves carefully. There's honey folded into the center of one of them. I'm not trusting you with another jar."

Kepi looked at the goat. The god Set was known to come in many forms: a hippo, a croc, even a pig. But most of all, he walked around with the head of a goat. Maybe she could frighten Menes into letting her out of the basket. "The god Set is going to protect us," she said boldly.

"There's bread soaked in beer for you. I didn't want you to dry out, but like I said, no jars till you act right."

"You should let us out onto the deck right now before you make the god Set madder. He can be frightful."

"And I saved you a chunk of oryx meat in there."

"You better listen, Menes. The god Set has taken the form of this goat."

Menes laughed. "You think a god would appear as a

small nanny? Look at her. Just eat, all right?"

Kepi sighed in defeat as Menes shut the lid. She didn't bother to push up against it. She sat on the bottom of the basket and looked around. Gradually her eyes adjusted to what little light there was.

Just then the nanny squatted her rear and emitted a steamy, smelly, noisy stream of urine.

Babu gave a little scream of surprise.

"You are a very bad man, Menes," shouted Kepi, pressing herself to the side away from the nanny. But she knew he couldn't hear her. She put her mouth to the hole in the basket. "You are a very bad man, Menes," she shouted again.

Babu pulled her hair.

"You have to find a better way of saying you're hungry," mumbled Kepi.

Baaa! Naaaa! Naaaa!

"So, little nanny, you got stolen, too." She pulled Babu off her head and set him on the basket bottom, holding him there with her left hand. With her right hand, she grabbed a goat teat and tugged, so the milk squirted in Babu's face. Babu snorted. Kepi pushed him closer. "Open your mouth." She squirted him again. This time she heard soft slurpy sounds.

"Honey for dessert." Kepi fed Babu the honey. Then she ate her own beer-soaked bread. She crawled around, trying to find a dry place to stretch out.

The nanny nosed her and nibbled on the hem of her dress.

"Stop it. I love this dress."

The nanny stamped and gave a high-pitched sneeze.

Kepi sat straight up. That goat sneezed! Sneezing was the mark of the gods' oracles. "Can you tell the future?"

The nanny walked around the basket bottom, stepping over Kepi and Babu. Finally she plopped down on Kepi's legs.

"All right," said Kepi. "You're no oracle. You're an ordinary goat, and you don't want to sleep in your mess. We don't either, right, Babu? But you can't sleep on me."

The nanny didn't budge. Babu chattered his teeth from his spot on her chest. Kepi realized that she was talking to a goat and a baby baboon as though they were people. But somehow it helped. It made her feel less alone.

"Go to sleep," said Kepi. "Both of you. It's night, and the boat won't get moving again till morning. And they won't open the lid till we're back out on the open river. So just sleep. We'll all be happier if we sleep through it." She closed her eyes and tried to imagine the soothing lights in the skies that usually put her to sleep. But she couldn't do it. So she sang. She started with the songs of the workers in the fields. Those were the ones she knew best, for she'd heard them all her life. Then she went on to the love songs that Nanu had taught her. Nanu had learned them from her friend's big sister. This was good; Kepi felt like Nanu was in the basket with her, singing silently.

Finally she fell silent herself.

That was when the little grinding noise started. Kepi knew instantly what it was; she'd spent a lot of time around goats. "Do you have to chew your cud in your sleep?" The nanny kept grinding. Babu whimpered. He was asleep, Kepi was sure, but he whimpered anyway. Kepi opened her eyes and stared into the dark. "At least we're not starving," she whispered to no one.

14
STORIES

Sunlight slanted in through the open lid and woke them. Menes looked in.

Kepi sat up and pushed the nanny off her. She glared up at Menes.

"What, no cheery morning greeting from you?" asked Menes.

"The nanny took care of her needs in the basket."

"I can smell that."

"So you have to let us out. All three of us."

"Can't do it. You've got to stay out of sight. We're stopping awhile to trade here. Then at midday, we'll cross the river to Nekheb to trade there."

"I thought this town was Nekheb."

"No, this is Nekhen."

"Towns shouldn't have names that differ by only one sound."

Menes smiled. "They're both the home of the goddess Nekhbet. Anyway, Nekheb is only a little farther north on the east bank. It's got the best pottery in this part of Egypt, and this part of Egypt has the best pottery in the country. If you weren't such a little troublemaker, you could come with me and see the huge kilns and even choose which pots we should trade for. I would let you swim in their sacred lake. Too bad you're so silly."

"I am not silly," shouted Kepi.

Menes lifted an eyebrow. "They make good beads there, too. I just might buy a bead necklace, and if you're very good, very very good, I might give it to you."

"Do you really think I want a necklace from you?"

"I never met anyone who cared as little about jewelry as you do."

This was not true. Kepi loved jewelry. She loved to dance and make music with her jewelry. But she was glad Menes thought she didn't. She wanted him to know nothing about her.

"Anyway," said Menes, "here's honey for the baboon and beer-soaked bread for you."

"I want lettuce," said Kepi, mostly just to be difficult.

Menes smiled proudly. "Funny you say that. I've got chicory."

"Chicory isn't the same thing as lettuce."

"It's close enough. You and the goat can share." He handed Kepi a cloth satchel. "And here." He lowered in a wooden bucket of river water with a rope. "Keep that goat drinking so her milk doesn't dry up." He shut the basket lid.

This day was beginning badly.

After a long while the basket jerked, and Kepi could feel the motion of the boat. "We're leaving Nekhen," she said aloud. "We're going to Nekheb. Maybe we'll also go to Nekhep and Nekhem and Nekhet. Do you think there really are cities with those names?" She giggled. But then she pressed her lips together in worry. "Sorry, great goddess Nekhbet. If you're bored enough to be listening to a girl stuck in a basket with a goat and a baboon, please forgive me. I'm not making fun of towns sacred to you. I'm just trying to keep from going crazy inside here." Kepi clapped her hands to try to clear the air. It didn't work.

"What shall we do?" she said out loud. "Tell me a story, Babu. Like Father used to do. How about something about the god Babi, with the baboon head? And you, Nanny, lecture me about the gods' rules. Like Mother used to do. Your lectures had better be about the god Set, since your head is like his. Go on, talk talk talk. Ha!"

Babu burped in his sleep. Nanny chewed her cud.

So Kepi did the talking. She dredged up every story she could, no matter how distant the memory. There were so many of them. And slowly she actually felt better. The stories seemed to hold her up. That must have been how the sun god Ra felt in the very beginning of everything, when there was nothing but the watery chaos called Nu. The god Ra rose up all on his own, just because he wanted to, and he created a hill to stand on, and then the world could begin. The god Ra pulled that hill out of his own mouth. That part of the tale had never made sense to Kepi before, but now it did. It made perfect sense. Kepi had to hold on to the stories. They came out of her mouth; they were her hill to stand on in the middle of this watery chaos. She had to be strong willed, like Ra.

The boat moved smoothly through the water. Ten men rowing at the sides and two more at the steering oars made for a lot of force; even without seeing the land go by, Kepi knew they were moving swiftly. Before long, she felt them slow down. Then came the bump that meant they'd docked.

15
SICK

Kepi stood in the basket, looking east out over the river, across the plains, to the distant limestone hills that ran from north to south as far as she could see. She turned her head west and saw the same thing in the distance. It seemed Egypt had stone walls down both sides, with the tops forming sand-covered plateaus. Every morning those western walls were flushed with sunrise; every evening those eastern walls were flushed with sunset. And all day long they were white white white. Though the sight was monotonous, Kepi loved those walls, for she imagined them working hard, trying to hold back the red desert. It was important to work hard to fight off things that would destroy you. Kepi looked to the walls for courage; her life was a constant fight. And it was only the stories about the gods that kept her sane. She cherished those stories.

Kepi hated living in the prison of this basket. But every day she reminded herself many times that it was worth it. This basket was carrying her to the capital. To the pharaoh.

That, too, would be a fight. No one could expect the pharaoh to just listen sweetly. Adults never seemed to do that. But Kepi would win; she had as strong a will as the god Ra; she would save her family.

She'd lost count of the number of days she'd been on the boat. Was it eight? Nine? It felt so long.

They'd stopped at two more cities.

The first was Ta-senet, where the crew picked up pottery again. Menes said they had to, because Ta-senet was the true home of pottery. The ram-headed god Heka had fashioned the very first humans from the Nile mud there by making pottery figures. In Kepi's village the old potter still coiled and pinched pots, but his son used the modern potter's wheel so he could make many more pots quickly. The god Heka made humans long before the potter's wheel, though. It must have taken him years to make enough humans to start the whole world. Kepi wished she could have seen the god Heka's kilns; she saw nothing of the cities from inside the basket.

But Menes told her Ta-senet was sacred to the goddess Nit. So Kepi had breathed in hope. She had been telling herself stories about all the gods, but she'd told lots and lots about Nit, in particular, since finding Babu in the first place had happened because of Nit's click beetle. That meant Kepi felt especially close to the goddess Nit by then, and somehow she was convinced the goddess Nit felt the same way. While the crew did their trading in Ta-senet, Kepi sat within the dark confines of the basket and prayed to Nit, over and over. She'd prayed a lot in her life, but not like this. This was quiet, almost like talking to a dear friend. *Please, great goddess Nit, please see me in this basket. Please help me get out of it.* Nit didn't answer, but that didn't matter. She was listening; that conviction alone made Kepi feel better.

The second town was Inr-ti, nestled between two hills. They picked up even more pottery there, because the town was famous for its black-topped pots, and they stored them in the other big baskets, with long grasses cushioning them. Menes told her that the river made a big turn there, so the water slowed and crocodiles gathered. That's why Inr-ti was sacred to the crocodile-headed god Sobek. What good news! All the gods were related to each other in one way or another, and the god Sobek was the child of the goddess Nit. Kepi had been thinking about this fact during her long hours in the basket. The click beetle had led her to the crocodile, and the crocodile had killed Babu's mother, so that's how Kepi got Babu. As she saw it, the goddess Nit and her son the god Sobek had worked together to give

Babu to Kepi. Or if not that, then at least they knew that Babu was with her and they knew what good care Kepi took of Babu. So that had to mean the god Sobek was Kepi's friend, too. While the crew traded in Inr-ti, Kepi found herself praying quietly again, to Sobek. *Please help me when we get to Ineb Hedj. And help me now as we travel. Help me get out of this basket. I feel so sick. I feel sick almost all day long.*

On the second night in Inr-ti, Menes told Kepi he had walked past a temple to the goddess Hathor. Kepi's spirits leaped at that news. Things were getting better and better! Hathor was the goddess of music and dance and moonlight. She was the one with the wonderful tinkling necklace. Kepi had prayed to her once long ago, asking her to make Mother allow her to wear her jewelry into the fields. Hathor hadn't answered that time. But much later, when Kepi first came into this basket, she had felt Hathor's moonglow caressing her. She was in a poppy seedpod haze then, to be sure. But still, the glow she felt had to have come from Hathor. Hathor might somehow care about Kepi. So that second night docked at Inr-ti, Kepi hugged her knees to her chest, even the hurt knee, and sang to Hathor. Her songs were prayers in a way, not asking for anything specific, but just a hope for strength. Hathor understood, Kepi was sure.

They were now on their way to the town of Djerty,

on the east bank. Menes hadn't yet told her what god Djerty was sacred to, but as soon as he did, Kepi would pray to him. Even if she couldn't see any particular connection to him, she'd pray. Prayer made her feel better.

Kepi had figured out the pattern of the crew. They'd travel in daylight, leaving one town early in the morning and arriving at the next by the afternoon. Then they'd dock for the night and trade all the next day, and stay at dock a second night. Then it was on to the next town. What that meant to her was a day with her poking out of the basket from the shoulders up, her face into the blessed wind carrying away the goat stink of the basket, then a night, a day, and another night closed in the basket, the only interruptions being Menes's ugly head as he handed her food or refilled the water bucket. And Menes's head was even uglier than it had been, because he'd gotten his hair cut short at Nekhen. He said the barbers there were particularly skilled. The crew must have agreed with him, for all of them had had their hair cut; all of them looked extra ugly.

The days when they were out on the center of the river, Menes let her sit on the deck. Sometimes, anyway. It was a relief to look at all the islands in the wide river, with their thick plant growth and singing birds. Now that Kepi's knee had healed, she could walk around a bit, too. But the man with the half ear always made her get back in the basket before long, and it was taking its toll on her. The anticipation of having to go inside the basket, of being cut off from seeing anything, made her shake. The whole world shrank when she was inside the basket. She could hardly catch her breath.

"I'm sick," she mumbled.

"Yes," came a voice from nowhere. "You can't stay in that festering basket."

Kepi wiped at her mouth. "Who said that?"

But no one was looking at her.

16
CROC

Babu was up on the mast. Whenever Kepi called to him, he clambered down instantly. But she didn't call him often, because she knew how much he enjoyed perching there. He must have suffered from the long hours closed in the basket even more than Kepi did. She blew him kisses often, even though she knew the wind carried them away before he could catch them. Nanny stood on the deck under him, with a large stack of acacia branches in front of her. She nibbled away at the leaves.

Kepi tipped her head back to see Babu, and she tottered. She felt woozy. She leaned forward, but that meant putting her head into the basket again, and the stench nearly made her faint. Her stomach retched dry. *Please help me. Somebody, help me.*

Bark! Bark bark bark!

Kepi looked up. It was Babu, barking like mad. Kepi had never heard Babu bark before. It was almost like a dog yap. Even in her weakened state, it alarmed her.

It must have alarmed Nanny, too, because she stamped and gave that high-pitched sneeze she always made when she felt jumpy. The combination of bark and sneeze set Kepi on edge; it felt like bad news was coming.

Babu looked ahead and showed his teeth and protruded his lower lip, curling it down and out, so that the pink inside showed. It was a terrible grimace. And Kepi knew immediately that Babu was afraid. She looked in the direction Babu's head was facing.

Swimming toward the boat was a crocodile. He held himself high in the water, so that his entire length showed, from the tip of his pointed snout to the tip of his tail. He was as long as four men lying in a line! Kepi had never seen a crocodile that long. She had never heard of a crocodile that long. It was terrifying. But at the same time it seemed magical, mystical. Godlike. Kepi gaped, amazed.

The crocodile slapped his snout on the river surface and blew water in a high fountain out of his nostrils. He roared.

"Croc!" went up the cry among the crew. They quickly rowed toward the far side of the river. That's how they'd avoided other floating crocodiles this morning. None of them had given chase.

But this one did. And Kepi knew he would. She burned with that knowledge. He veered their way without slowing down. The powerful slow swish of his tail fascinated her. His tail alone could turn over an ordinary boat. She watched in stunned horror.

"He's coming straight at us!" someone screamed.

The crocodile opened his jaws wide and came fast in a flurry of spray. Kepi couldn't take her eyes off those long, sharp teeth. It didn't make sense; she shouldn't be seeing teeth now. Crocodiles didn't attack openmouthed like that. They sunned themselves openmouthed. They sat patiently while plovers ate from between their gigantic teeth, always openmouthed. But they didn't attack openmouthed till the very last few seconds.

Could it really be the god Sobek? But no. Even if Sobek had heard her prayers, gods didn't show themselves for ordinary people like Kepi. It was just coincidence that the crocodile came right after Kepi had prayed for help.

"Smack him on the head!" shouted one of the men at the steering oars.

Two men ran to the side with oars ready.

But at the last minute, the crocodile dove. Seconds later, the boat was rocked from beneath.

"He's attacking the hull!"

"Crazy croc!"

Baskets slid from side to side. Babu came hurtling down from the mast and leaped onto Kepi's head. Nanny clambered onto a box beside Kepi's basket and stood up on her hind hooves. Kepi caught her forehooves and dragged her into the basket.

If the crocodile kept this up, the boat would come apart. And there were other crocodiles in the water—crocodiles who were definitely not gods, crocodiles who would eat them. Kepi held on to Babu with one hand and Nanny with the other.

The crew rowed as hard as they could. And the rocking finally stopped.

But almost instantly the crocodile resurfaced. He floated a moment, then swam fast.

"He's coming again!" shouted a man.

The crocodile swam right for the boat and rose up so his whole front half was out of the water. Kepi watched, terror stricken. His giant jaws snapped—open, shut—on the middle of an oar. The wood split with such force, the top half of the oar flew back and hit the rower in the head. He went flying into the river. The crocodile swam beside the boat for a minute, part of the oar still sticking out of his broad snout. His skin was pale gray and green in the sunlight. The pupils of his eyes had narrowed to thin black slits in a ball of yellow. He slapped the boat with his tail, then dove.

They all stared in shock at the surface of the river. The water was opaque. They could only imagine what it hid. The man didn't come back up. The crocodile didn't come back up.

One of the two men who normally steered ran over to the empty bench. "I'll row. One's enough to steer. Let's go! Now!"

The men rowed in perfect unison, fast and hard.

Kepi looked back in desperation. *Please, man,* she prayed in her heart, *come back up. Come back up!* He couldn't die. No one should die. She didn't wish ill on these men; she just wanted them to treat her better. *Please, great god Sobek, please don't let that man die. If that crocodile was you, please push him up. Let him swim to the boat. Please.* But nothing came to the surface of the water.

This was horrible. What would happen to the man's body if he died? How could his family ever mourn him properly? His poor *ka* would never be honored, never find peace.

Kepi looked around at the crew. Their jaws were set; their eyes glittered with fear. And in that moment she realized: She should speak up now, before they calmed down. She shouldn't let the moment pass. "That crocodile was the god Sobek!" shouted Kepi, only half believing herself. "He's mad because you're not supposed to keep us locked up in this basket. We're getting sick in here. You have to let us out on deck."

No one answered her.

"It's the truth! Inr-ti is sacred to Sobek. I prayed to him when we were docked there. He heard me. He came to tell you. It's a message."

The half-ear man looked at Menes. He sneered and shook his head.

Menes rushed over and hissed in Kepi's ear, "Shut your mouth. One of our men died back there. Stop talking nonsense, or everyone's going to get mad at you."

"I didn't pray for anyone to die," Kepi whispered back. "I swear. I just prayed for help. I have to get out of this basket, Menes. I'm sick."

"I'll figure out something. Just shut your mouth. Not one more word about the gods." Menes went back to his rowing bench.

They rowed hard for a long time, and no one talked.

Gradually Kepi's heartbeat slowed again. Gradually she could think straight. No crocodile would have acted like that. She put her hands to her cheeks and held them there as if to steady herself. What she had said was true; it had to have been Sobek. He came to Kepi's rescue.

But even if that was true, he hadn't helped her get out of the basket.

And that man had gone under the water.

Things were worse now. Far worse.

17

HIPPO

Kepi's thoughts jumbled around. It had been a terrible mistake to beg the gods to interfere. Now the crew blamed her for that lost man. They were even more set against her. Not a single one looked at her. She felt chilled all over. She hugged herself. If she had to sleep in the basket one more night, she thought she might die.

Babu barked. Nanny sneezed. Kepi clutched the edge of the basket.

"What's that?" One of the men stood up. "Hippos. Look."

Ahead on the right were many hippopotamuses. Most of them stood in the shallows near the bank, just lolling in the waters, but several swam with only the tops of their heads and their nostrils showing. At home Kepi loved the sight of hippopotamuses, especially their funny round ears and wide, shiny backs. She liked how the mothers were so affectionate to their babies. There were lots of babies in this pod. Cute, with their rolls of fat around their necks. Big happy families. Kepi had to squeeze her eyes shut for a moment, she missed her family so much.

"Hippos are worse than crocodiles," said one of the men.

"No, they're not. They don't eat people."

"They turn over boats and drown them. That's just as bad."

"We'll be all right so long as we don't rile them. We've passed hippos before. Lots of times. You're just upset because of that monster croc. But he was crazy. That never should have happened. He was just plain crazy."

"Right," said the man at the steering oar. "Hippos are nothing. We'll give them wide berth. It won't be a problem."

The men rowed hard, and the man at the rear steered the boat straight down the center of the river, where the current was strongest. But oh, one hippo came swimming at them determinedly, foam rising around him like a cloud.

No! This couldn't be happening again. *No!* Kepi stared; that hippo was definitely coming fast and furious. He was so big, he set up waves in his wake. *Go back,* Kepi prayed. *Please, please go back.*

"He's a giant."

"The biggest bull I've ever seen."

"Another monster!"

"He's coming right for us."

The hippopotamus rammed the boat on the right side near the front. The blow was so strong, the bow of the boat lifted out of the water and came slapping back down with a huge splash that soaked everyone. Boxes went crashing against one another. Baskets tumbled onto their sides. Babu clung to Kepi's head and neck so tight, she had trouble seeing and breathing, but she managed to hold fast to Nanny's neck anyway. The three of them went skidding out of their toppled basket and slammed into the mast.

Kepi heard a hiss: *sssssssset*. The god Set!

Then came a snort and a second enormous blow, stronger than the first. The splash that followed was denser than the heaviest rainfall Kepi had ever been in. Men screamed. Babu and Nanny and Kepi went careening across the boat the other way now, slammed up against a rower's bench. Everything tumbled and tossed.

Gradually, though, the boat stopped rocking. No more blows came. The hippopotamus had gone away.

Without a word, the men took their places at the benches and rowed. But now there were only three at each side and one man at the rear. Four more men had disappeared under the water.

Kepi stared at the surface behind them, willing those men to pop up. But they didn't. Maybe they couldn't swim. Maybe they got conked on the head in all that tossing and sank straight down. Maybe things hidden under the water had gotten them.

Tears blurred Kepi's eyes. She hadn't intended her prayers to the gods to have such hateful effects. These men had done a very wrong thing. They had stolen her, when it was illegal to steal an Egyptian girl. They had stolen Babu, too. They intended to trade away both of them. That was wrong, but not so wrong that any of them should have died. The god Set had been cruel. Kepi brushed at her tears, but they kept coming for a long time.

The men rowed, and Kepi studied their faces. They looked straight ahead. But she could see they were shaken. Probably nothing this bad had ever happened to any of them before. She had to try to find a way to make things better.

Lots of baskets had been lost. Kepi's basket was still there, though. It had gotten hooked on a harpoon. She unhooked it and righted it. But she didn't climb in.

Broken pottery pieces littered the deck. Kepi walked around, tossing them into the water. At least this way no one would get cut. A box had gotten bashed open against one of the benches. The copper chest inside it was exposed. Its top had been twisted askew. Kepi opened the top, to try to straighten it. Inside the chest was a mound of gold and, even more precious, silver. Most of the pieces were just lumps of the raw metals. But there were several flat ingots and cups of coiled silver.

No one Kepi knew had gold or silver. But she'd seen these valuable foreign metals in the jewelry worn by rich people in the city of Wetjeset-Hor, near her village. That gold came from Nubia, in the south. And Father had seen a lot of silver and gold when he was up north, because he had visited Ineb Hedj. He said these metals were imported to that city from places far away, Minos and Mun-digak and the land of the Hattians. So no matter what, these were foreign metals. What were they doing here, in this chest?

Kepi looked around. No one seemed to be watching her. She quickly slipped a single piece of silver into her mouth. It sat heavy on her tongue. She knew it was wrong. But silver might be able to pay her and Babu's passage back home from Ineb Hedj. And she wouldn't need to do that in the first place if these men hadn't stolen her. So really, even though she had her own reasons for being on this journey now, really it was only right that they should pay for her to get back home.

She carefully worked at the hinges on the chest until

she finally bent them enough that the lid closed again. She carried the chest to the center of the deck, where it would be safe. And she went on with her job of cleaning up the aftermath of the hippopotamus attack.

18
LOSS

They pulled the boat over to the shore and anchored. The crew formed a circle and sat down on the deck.

A man shook his head and wiped his mouth. "What can we do for them? We've got to do something."

"We'll be at Djerty soon." Another man pointed. The outermost buildings of the town could be seen not far up the river.

"Nah, it's best to do it now."

So they talked about the five men who had gone under the water. They said their names and whatever they knew about their families or where they were from. It wasn't much. The men had come together on this big trade boat for the work. They hadn't known one another beforehand, and they never intended to see one another afterward. Still, they had been together all day long, all night long, during this journey; they had developed strong bonds. Some of them cried.

"What about their things?"

"We can't go back and deliver them now."

"If we throw them into the water here, there's a chance they'll find them."

So they gathered any personal things that remained on board that had belonged to the lost men. They tossed it all overboard, for use in the afterlife.

"At least their *kas* will have sustenance for all eternity. They can eat fish."

The others murmured agreement.

Then someone said, "That was no ordinary crocodile."

Up to this point, Kepi had been sitting motionless beside Nanny at the bow of the deck with Babu on her head, outside the circle of men, completely stilled by the sadness of it all. But now she nervously petted Nanny's ear with one hand and Babu's tail with the other. She studied the men's faces. They wouldn't look at her. They'd never looked at her much, but now they wouldn't look at her at all. Her mouth went dry.

"He was bigger than other crocs. Lots bigger. Like some magic thing."

"And he came at us in the middle of the day, for no reason. We didn't have meat or fish hanging off the side of the boat. No one was dangling an arm or leg in the water. No reason. No reason at all."

"The god Sobek sent him."

"Or maybe it really was Sobek himself."

"It's like the girl said. She prayed to Sobek, and look what happened."

Menes twisted the tips of his beard. "I told her Inr-ti was sacred to Sobek. She didn't know on her own. She's just a little village girl. She knows nothing. I won't tell her about the gods of the towns we go to anymore. Not a word."

"But what about the hippo?"

"What about him?" asked Menes.

"Hippos aren't sacred to any of the gods of the towns we've been to, but he came after us all the same."

"That's right. We didn't do anything to annoy him. He just charged us."

"Hippos are the most dangerous animal of the Nile," said Menes. "We all know that."

"This one wasn't normal, the way he rammed twice, then stopped. It was like he wanted to hurt us, but not all of us."

"Not the girl." It was the man with the half ear. He glared at Kepi.

"It could have been another god in disguise."

"Maybe Set. He sometimes comes as a hippo."

"Oh! I heard him." One of the men slapped his forehead in recognition. "I heard him announce his name.

I forgot it in all the confusion till you said it now. But I heard the name *Set*."

Kepi bit her lip so hard, she tasted blood. Someone else had actually heard the hippo say he was Set. It was real—every last shred of doubt disappeared; the gods were with her.

"Set protects her!"

"Why, the girl doesn't need to pray to gods of the towns we visit. She can just pray to Set and we'll get attacked."

"How could the god Set care about a simple village girl?" Menes spread his hands palms upward in entreaty. "Come on, it was just a crazy hippo."

"Look at her name. You call her Kepi. She's a tempest. And Set's the god of storms. She's Set's girl, all right. He came to avenge her. And he'll come again."

"Yeah. He'll come again!"

"We can shake rattles at him. Rattles frighten Set."

"You really think that hippo would have been scared at a rattle?"

Half Ear shook his head. "He'll kill us all next time."

"All right, all right." Menes rubbed his hands together. "Listen. Most of the pottery we traded for was broken or fell in the river. We still have one chest of precious metals to trade, and we can bring back a decent load of pottery from it. But it's nothing compared to what we should have had. We need a way to make up for our losses. Am I right?"

The men grudgingly nodded.

"So the answer is the baboon and the girl. Selling them is our only way out of ruin."

"I'd rather be ruined than dead."

"Me, too."

"No one else has to die." Menes put his fists on his hips. "All we need is for the girl to want to come with us. Really want to come. If that happens, the gods won't have any reason to attack us anymore." Menes walked over to Kepi and took out his knife. He held it in front of her nose. "If you come with us willingly, I won't kill your baboon. But if at any point you resist or try to get others to help you or pray to the gods for help, I'll kill him."

Kepi shook her head in horrified disbelief. "You need Babu. To sell."

"Five men died. Think. You really want to take a risk on what I will or won't do?"

"You're awful." Kepi locked her eyes on Menes's. "But you're not that awful."

Menes went to the leather strop hanging from the mast and sharpened his knife.

Kepi closed her hand around Babu's tail. "All right. I won't pray to the gods anymore. But you have to be kind to us. All three of us."

"What does 'kind' mean?"

"We can't be locked in the basket anymore. And we get to come into town with you whenever we dock."

Menes shook his head. "Into town? I don't . . ."

"We get to come into town. That's the deal."

Menes looked around at the other men and nodded. The other men didn't nod back, but Menes kept nodding as though they were all agreeing. "All right. It's settled."

It wasn't even midday when they arrived in Djerty, it was so close to Inr-ti. Menes stepped off onto the dock, and Kepi went to follow, with Babu on her head and Nanny in tow.

"The goat stays," said one of the men.

"She needs exercise," said Kepi. "Besides, you agreed."

The man looked at Menes. "Is this girl in charge of us now?"

Menes stared at Kepi with a lowered brow.

"All right," said Kepi. It didn't matter. She would take Nanny for a walk later.

"Leave the baboon, too." This time it was Half Ear.

"No!"

"Someone might steal him off your head."

"Babu comes," said Kepi.

"I'll keep the girl with me at all times," said Menes. "No one will steal the baboon."

The man at the steering oar said, "Let's tie every-thing up and all go together to trade this chest of metals for as much pottery as we can get. Just fill her to the brim—and then not have to trade at all the rest of the way home. That way we can simply dock at night, and we don't have to go into towns at all—and we don't have to deal with this girl's nonsense."

"All of us? Who will guard the boat?"

"What's left to guard? No one's going to steal the whole boat. You'd need a crew to row it. And it will take all of us to carry back that much pottery."

And so the seven men trooped off, carrying the chest. Kepi walked in the center of them, with Babu on her head. She waved to Nanny, who was left behind, tied to the mast.

Djerty was a smaller town than Wetjeset-Hor. But it clearly had some rich people, judging from the jewelry of those who passed them.

They went straight to a pottery workshop. Within the hour, they had traded gold and silver for a boatload of pottery. Then they went to a basket workshop and bought enough to hold all the pots. After that, it was a matter of several trips back and forth from the work-shops to the dock to fill the boat. The potter's helpers joined in carrying the largest vessels. No one asked Kepi to carry anything. That was good, because she still felt ill. Sometimes chills hit her so hard, her teeth chattered.

When they finished, it was the middle of the afternoon. Half Ear said, "The rest of us will stay here now and rearrange the full baskets, so there's a better distribution of weight. Menes, you take the girl for a meal. When you get back, you'll guard the load, and the rest of us can go eat."

"Babu needs to eat now," said Kepi. "So I'll stay on the boat with Nanny."

Half Ear sneered at Kepi. Then he shrugged. He looked at Menes. "Go ahead. Bring back something for the girl, and it'll be our turn."

Kepi put Babu under Nanny, where he quickly latched onto a teat and nursed. She filled a bucket with river water and set it in front of Nanny, who, she had learned, liked to drink while Babu was nursing.

Menes was watching her, and Kepi knew it. She looked at him. He gave a small smile. Then he left.

No sooner had he disappeared down an alley than Half Ear grabbed Kepi from behind and clapped a hand over her mouth. She struggled, but he twisted her arm up behind her till she had to stand on tiptoe, and still it hurt so bad, she was screaming inside her heart. She tried not to move in the least, because every movement made the pain that much more excruciating.

"Listen, men. The gods protect this girl, not the

baboon. And we don't need her. A slave is worth nothing compared to a baboon. We'll trade for plenty from whatever temple takes him. She's nothing but trouble. I say we get rid of her."

Rid of her? Kepi felt woozy.

"Come on, Ptah. Menes won't like that."

Ptah. Horrible Half Ear had a regular name. Kepi wished she didn't know that. She hated him right now. It was like Father's proverb—she'd had her eye on the snake, and she'd missed the scorpion altogether.

"Yeah. Menes said we're not to hurt her. That's what he said, right at the start."

Menes said that? Kepi blinked. Really?

"And right at the start I said she'd be trouble, remember? I was right. Menes doesn't know anything. Besides, he won't be part of it. We'll do it and leave right now."

"Without him?"

"Yeah, without him! He's the one who got us into this mess."

"We can't travel on the river at night."

"If we row hard enough, we won't have to. We can make it to Waset before dark."

"You're right."

"Wait. I don't want to have any part in killing the girl."

Killing? Kepi's knees buckled.

"Me neither. What do you think the god Set would

do if we killed his girl?"

"Then we'll dump her somewhere alive. No one has a problem with that, right?"

"I don't know."

"I guess not."

"Throw that empty basket over the goat and the baboon, fast."

A man turned Kepi's giant basket upside down and closed in Nanny and Babu.

"Now get me some rope and a cloth."

Another man hurried over with a strip of cloth.

Ptah took his hand off Kepi's mouth to reach for the cloth, and she screamed. Something hit the back of her head, hard.

19
DITCHED

Kepi opened her eyes. It was dark, and she was lying on cold ground. She lifted her head to sit up and *clunk!* She fell back. Her forehead hurt. And now the back of her head really hurt—far worse than her forehead. She was under something. And her hands were tied behind her. And there was a gag in her mouth.

And now she remembered what had happened. They'd ditched her.

Wherever she was, she had to get out of here fast. She rolled onto her side. Her shoulder touched what was above her: stone. Homes and stores were made of mud bricks. Nothing was made of stone except a temple. Oh, no!

Forgive me, god or goddess, prayed Kepi inside her heart, *whatever god or goddess you are, forgive me for coming into your home. Ordinary people like me are not invited. I know that. I didn't come on my own. I was placed here by bad men. Forgive me. I will leave as*

fast as I can. With your help, of course. Thank you for
understanding.

"You haven't done anything wrong. It's all right."
The voice was real. And soothing.

Kepi waited, but no more words came. So she rolled
again. She was quickly out from under the thing. Her
eyes adjusted to the dim light of early evening. She had
been under a bench. And the side of it was inscribed.
She managed to sit up and then stand. It was hard to do
without the use of her hands.

There was no one there; no one who belonged to that
voice. Kepi didn't expect there would be.

This was a small chamber, not a temple at all. And
the walls were made of mud brick, not stone. Only the
inscribed bench was stone. There was a hole in one wall,
and a door in another. Kepi peeked through the hole. She
could make out a statue inside painted blue and red
and gold. What? This was a rich person's *mastaba*—
a burial tomb. And the *ka* of that person lived in the
statue. Kepi bowed in respect. She slowly backed away
and out the door. On the sides of and above the door
were stone slabs with more inscriptions and pictures in
bright colors. Kepi couldn't read, but she could tell from
the pictures that the deceased must have enjoyed fishing
and having women dance before him. From one picture,
she guessed he was probably the overseer of a building

project. Maybe even a temple. And he must have worshipped a bull-headed god. He was a big eater, too: the walls had carvings of all the foods he wanted in the afterlife.

She turned and walked as quickly as she dared down the closest street. She had to be careful, though, because she couldn't risk tripping or she'd fall flat on her face with her hands tied behind her like that. Shops had closed for the evening, and families were asleep. A dog barked as she walked past one home. That set up barking from lots of dogs in nearby homes. In the far distance, jackals howled back. Jackals. Even without the howling, it felt creepy to be out so late all alone. But that eerie noise made her frantic.

She couldn't stop herself from running now. She headed straight for the first open door she saw and went inside.

Men sat in pairs at tables here and there, playing a game on multicolored boards. One player moved ivory pieces around a board, and the other moved ebony ones. The air smelled strongly of beer.

Kepi stood inside the doorway and looked from man to man. One of them was missing a leg. Had a chunk of rock fallen on him, like the one that had fallen on Kepi's father? It must have been huge, to kill his whole leg. Maybe he had worked for Pharaoh Khufu on the pyramid, too, and maybe he'd gotten no help either. He was just as bad off as Father.

"What have we here?" A smiling man came up. His face was weather lined. He must have been old. "A little wild thing. You won't bite me if I take that gag off you, will you?"

Kepi shook her head.

The man untied her gag.

"They stole my baboon." The words burst out of her. "And the goat."

"Unusual words from an unusual critter," said the old man.

Right. Kepi had better talk sensibly. It was important these men believe her so they'd help her. She had to catch up with that trade boat. Babu was on it. And so was the silver piece that she'd taken from the chest. She'd hidden it between ropes at the base of the mast. That silver piece was her only way to trade for passage home after she talked to the pharaoh. "I need help. Please untie my hands."

The old man untied Kepi's hands. "I'll walk you home now, little beggar."

"I'm not a beggar. And you can't walk me home." Kepi's bottom lip trembled, but she fought off tears. "I live way down south. Near Wetjeset-Hor."

The old man looked around. "Anyone know where that is?"

"I do," said a man with a shaved head. "It's days and days south of here."

The old man frowned. "How did you get here, girlie?"

"I was . . ." She was about to say stolen, but then the men might decide to send her home rather than helping her get back on the boat. ". . . given a ride by men in a boat. But then they hit me on the head and tied me up and left me . . ." She didn't want to tell them about the *mastaba*, in case they got angry at her. " . . . and left me on the ground. They took the boat away, with my baboon and a goat. She's not my goat, but she's not really theirs either. They're not even nice to her."

"Seems there's a whole lot of stealing going on these days," said a man near the rear. "And a whole lot of strange talk about baboons."

"Did someone else talk about baboons?" asked Kepi, all at once hopeful.

"A drunk down at the dock."

It had to be Menes. He would want to catch up to the trade boat just as much as Kepi did. He was her best chance. Kepi blinked. "Which way's the dock?"

"Now now, we won't let you go running off to the dock," said the old man. "That dock's no place for a—"

But Kepi was already out the door. She ran straight down the street till it ended and she had to turn.

Randomly, she turned right and ran and ran and ran. Finally the buildings ended and the road stopped. She was at the very edge of town, and she still couldn't see the river. The river was to the west, she knew that much. But she didn't know how to tell which way was west from the night sky. She'd only been out at night with Father, and always in the hot months. And that's when it was light out a little longer, so she rarely was awake long enough to see the full range of lights in the sky. The lights grouped in different places this time of year, anyway.

She remembered the jackals howling. Lions could be out there, too. And leopards. She had to think straight. There must be a way to figure out which road led to the docks.

But she obviously couldn't think straight, because no solution came to her. All right, then, she would just walk back to the first street cutting off this one and take it all the way to the end, and if that didn't work, then the second street, and so on. And that's what she did. Moonlight guided her steps; she never fell, not once.

It was the middle of the night before Kepi came out on the docks. At last: There was Menes, sprawled on the ground and reeking of beer. She stood over him a moment. He looked pitiful and almost small, all out in the open like this. But he also looked kind of sweet. Or maybe that was just because a strong feeling of tenderness had come over her. This man had problems with his thinking. He had intended to sell her as a slave—so there was a hole in his heart. But at the same time, she now knew he'd looked out for her with the crew. In his own odd way, he might very well be a friend. And right now he was the only friend she had. She might be the only friend he had, too.

There was no point waking him; travel on the river was impossible at night. And the way his mouth hung open, she didn't think he was wakeable, anyway.

Kepi sat up against Menes and looked at the vast sky. At least she could fall asleep watching the distant lights, like she always did back home. A sharp pang of longing for home made her whole body hurt. She could hardly bear to think about Father and Mother and Nanu. They must worry about her all the time.

The stars were exceptionally glorious right then, twinkling and shimmering in a big swath from one horizon to the other. On a night like this, Nanu and Kepi would have basked in the glory of the sky and sung together till one of them dozed off. Had Nanu watched these stars tonight and fallen asleep wondering where her little sister was, whether she was even alive? Did she cry? Did they all cry?

Kepi was crying now. She would get home. She had a job to do in Ineb Hedj first. An important job. The sight of that man with the missing leg in the game hall had reminded her how important it was. But as soon as she'd done it, she would get back to her family. Fast.

Disappearance was brutal. Maybe more brutal than knowing something awful had happened to someone. She wouldn't leave her family wondering forever.

The families of those men who had died today, they'd suffer from their disappearance. They'd wonder forever. Kepi could almost hear their wailing in her heart. She was very sad for them.

And she was sad for herself: Babu was gone. Loss made every part of her ache. Kepi stared up at the sky. *Please, whatever god is watching me, please make the crew treat Babu and Nanny well.*

The sliver of moonlight was delicate and kind. "I will," came the gentle voice, the same voice she'd heard when she was in the *mastaba*.

And she almost expected it. Life had become so much confusion, but one little part made sense now: The gods really did watch and listen. They talked to her. And they came in the form of animals. "You helped me find Menes, didn't you?" Kepi whispered. "You made the alleys light up, even though there's hardly a moon at all tonight. You lit my way. Thank you, great goddess Hathor."

Despite how sick and sad Kepi felt, determination blanketed her. She would make it to Ineb Hedj. And she'd get Menes to help her. Then she'd go home and never leave her family again.

20
INSULTS

"What?" Someone yanked on Kepi's arm. She opened her eyes with difficulty—it had taken her a long time to fall asleep—and looked up into the gawking face of Menes, leaning over her. "You're here? You're here!" He danced in a circle, shaking his fists at the sky, while she managed to sit up. "Hurrah!" And he stopped. He leaned over again and clapped her on the back. "So where's the baboon?"

"They stole him."

Menes's eyes widened and his fingers tightened around Kepi's shoulder. "How could you let them do that?"

"I didn't let them. And don't yell at me. You let them, too."

Menes dropped down on the ground beside her. He cupped his forehead in his hands and rocked his head, as though it was as heavy as a boulder.

Babu was gone and Kepi was hungry and she felt all strange and nothing was right. "We should find a family to take us in for a while."

"Don't be absurd. We can't waste time here."

Kepi didn't want to waste time either. But she felt so sick. "I'll pray to the gods."

"You little faker. The gods didn't help you. You just took advantage of the moment to get your freedom from the basket."

"That's not true."

"Oh, yeah? If the gods protected you, how come you wound up in our boat to start with, huh?"

Kepi turned her head away. It was true. The gods had let the men steal her. But she was sure things had changed. She was close to the gods now. They had to care about her, too. It was impossible not to care about someone who cared about you.

"It doesn't make sense," said Menes. "And you know it as well as I do. Some god may have sent that crazy croc and that crazy hippo. But whatever god it was, he sure wasn't looking out for you. I'm not stupid."

Gods could be mysterious—everyone knew that. Just because she didn't understand, just because Menes didn't understand, didn't mean that the gods weren't with her. Kepi squared her jaw at him. "You got left behind. You look stupid to me."

Menes glared at her. "I don't take well to insults. And I just had a very bad night. So, little tempest, you're on your own." He stood up and brushed himself off. "That's my baboon. I'm going after them." He walked up the street toward town.

Kepi jumped to her feet. "Wait! I'm coming with you!" But Menes turned a corner. He was out of sight already. Kepi gulped. Then fury hit her. She couldn't believe Menes had called Babu his baboon. He really was awful. Let him go.

Kepi wiped her nose, which was running. Her throat was sore, too. She'd caught a cold overnight. A cold, on top of being sick from the basket. At least on the boat Nanny and Babu and Kepi had kept each other warm as they slept; nothing had warmed her last night. Every time she had snuggled against Menes, he had groaned and rolled away.

She looked down at herself. Her dress was dirty. No, it was worse than that. It was filthy. Mother would have been ashamed. She kept her family immaculately clean, as any Egyptian mother did. Kepi's stomach cramped from emptiness. The morning chill hadn't burned off yet; she shivered. She rubbed at her nose again. Now her hand was revoltingly snotty. She wiped it on her dress. What did it matter? She was quickly becoming a slimy mess.

Kepi cried.

When her tears finally seemed to run out, she washed her face in the river. Hunger seized her. She hadn't eaten since yesterday morning. She couldn't wait for Menes to come back; she had better go find him. Somehow he always had food.

She walked into town. Smells of the morning meal came from open windows and doors everywhere. Kepi licked her lips and kept walking. She looked down every side street. She peeked into a brewery. No Menes.

She leaned into an open door. A woman was cleaning tables with a cloth. It was an eating hall. Maybe if Kepi looked pathetic enough, this woman would have pity on her and give her a crust of bread, at least. "Excuse me, please." Kepi used her sweetest voice. "I'm . . . I'm sort of lost. I mean, I lost my food satchel."

The woman turned, took one look at Kepi, and gasped. She ran at her and snapped the cloth in her face. "Get out of here. Go, before I sic a dog on you."

Kepi backed out and walked to the corner. She turned right and staggered.

Dizziness made her rest against a wall and lean over. The area behind her eyes hurt now. And the area between her eyes. She wasn't chilly anymore. She was hot. That was how colds were—they got worse fast.

Kepi walked as fast as she could manage to the dock. Menes had to come back there soon. He'd take care of her.

The dock had transformed since she'd woken up. All the fishing boats had gone out. Only two little reed boats were tied there, side by side. Both were empty. Exhaustion overcame Kepi. She climbed into a boat and stretched out on the bottom. She closed her eyes against the rude sun. The bobbing of the boat on the water soothed her. She fought to stay awake.

"All right, then" came a voice, soon enough. "It's a deal."

Kepi opened her eyes and pushed herself up to sitting. Menes was climbing into the reed boat beside the one she was in. A man stood on the dock and handed him two paddles and a pole.

"Menes!"

"It's you." He put down the gear and shook his head.

"I'm sick."

Menes furrowed his brow and peered hard at her. "Well, don't bother me about it. I've just lost the results of several months of work. You know what that means?"

"You're ruined."

"Ruined? Don't be an idiot. I only talked about ruin with the crew to persuade them to do things my way. But I can always get along. I'm mad, that's what I am. No one gets away with stealing from me. I'm going to get my baboon back. You live in the other direction. I'm not helping you get home."

"I don't want to go home. I want to go with you."

"Really?" Menes dipped a bucket over the side of the

boat and filled it with water. He set it in the bottom of his boat. "Why?"

"I have something I have to do in Ineb Hedj."

"What?"

"Talk to the pharaoh."

Menes dropped his head toward Kepi. Then he laughed. "You know, I half believe you. You're something, all right. It just might be a good idea to take you. You could help with paddling. But you have to say sorry for insulting me."

"You're the one who insults me," said Kepi.

Menes untied the rope that held the little boat to the dock post. He was really leaving. Without her. He sat in the middle of the boat and stuck his paddle in the water, maneuvering the boat backward, away from the dock.

Kepi stood up in her boat. "I'm sorry. I won't insult you anymore."

"Promise?"

"Yes." Kepi splayed her legs to keep from wobbling. "But you have to promise you won't call Babu your baboon anymore."

Menes was already out in the river. "All right, little tempest. If you can catch this, you can come." He threw the rope toward her.

Kepi jumped for it. Both the rope and Kepi landed in the water. She came up spluttering.

Menes paddled over and held out the wooden blade to her. She grabbed hold and he pulled her on board. "Are you too sick to paddle?"

Kepi's teeth chattered and she thought she was going to vomit. But she pushed her sopping hair out of her eyes and picked up the second paddle.

"All right, then." Menes moved more toward the rear.

Kepi sat in front of him and dipped her paddle into the opposite side.

"Do it this way," said Menes. And he taught her to grip it firmly, dip it in straight down beside her, push it straight back as far as she could reach, then lift it out just enough to clear the surface of the water as she swung it back around to dip in beside her and start all over again.

After a while, Kepi found the rhythm natural. It was hard work, but she could do it fine. "How did you manage to get this boat?"

"I bought it. I kept a few nuggets of silver from the chest. Always keep a reserve. That's my advice."

That was like Father, when he said to put by for a rainy day. Well, Kepi had done that—she'd taken that one silver piece from the trunk. But she'd been stupid to hide it on the boat. Menes was trickier than her. Everyone was so tricky. It made Kepi tired to think about it. "How long will it take us to get to Waset?"

"We can be there by tonight."

Finally, good news. Tonight Kepi could hold Babu again.

They paddled a long time. When the sun was directly overhead, Menes laid his paddle in the bottom of the boat. "We can let the current carry us awhile. Go on, put your paddle down."

Kepi laid her paddle on her side of the bottom. Then she turned around to face Menes, and she fell backward. She didn't even try to push herself up again.

"You really are sick." Menes opened a cloth satchel. "Here." He came over beside her and lifted her head and shoulders up. He held a jar to her mouth. "Drink this."

The beer was cool and delicious. Kepi wiped her mouth. "Thanks."

Menes eased her back down and handed her a hunk of bread. "Eat slowly." He ate and drank himself and watched her. "You remind me of someone."

"Your sister Nanu?"

Menes laughed. "I don't have a sister Nanu. I just said that to make you trust me."

Kepi let out a little cry of dismay. "Do you ever tell the truth?"

"When it suits me. I just figured out who you remind me of—myself. You're my stubborn little tempest."

Kepi rolled onto her side with her back to him and gnawed on the bread. "I can't wait to hold Babu tonight."

"You won't see him tonight."

Kepi held on to the side of the boat and pulled herself up to sitting. "You said we'd be in Waset tonight—and I heard the men say they were going to Waset."

"Sure. That's where they spent last night, I bet. But they traded away all the gold and silver. And they have a boat full of pottery already. They don't need to stay in towns any longer than to sleep. By now, they're half-way to Nubt—the next town. They'll stay ahead of us the whole way to Ineb Hedj. Getting farther ahead all the time. If you paddle hard, you might see Babu in a month."

A month. Kepi curled into a ball with her head on her knees. A month without Babu. A month of Menes. A month of not seeing her family. And then all the time it would take to get home.

A month was an eternity.

21

THE RIVER

Kepi didn't know which day it happened, but one day she realized the paddle felt like an extension of her hands. Her neck and shoulders didn't hurt anymore. Her knees had grown thick calluses. She felt strong and healthy. They traveled all day, every day, and she could do it without a problem.

With health and strength, she could look around in delight again, for they passed so many wonderful things. Lots of different kinds of wading birds. Lazy crocs. And pods of hippos. None of them attacked, which Menes said was because they didn't mind the intrusion of the smaller boats. But just to be sure, they banged their paddles on the wooden part of the boat often so any hippos around would pop their eyes up above the water to see what was happening; that way Kepi and Menes knew where they were and could steer around them.

As they moved northward, the shores gradually grew greener, till they were thick with plants Kepi had never seen before. Still, the trees were familiar: mostly date palms and figs and sycamore figs. But they grew in clusters of many together, unlike in the south.

At night they slept in towns or in villages built into the hillsides. Kepi and Menes would carry their little boat to some house on the very edge of town, where the owner had agreed to let them lean it against a side wall. Usually they caught fish to cook in the homeowner's outdoor fireplace and share with his family. Both of them would do chores in exchange for bread and greens and sweet, thick, porridge-like beer. Then they'd sleep outdoors under their boat, with Kepi on the outside edge, so she could peek out at the lights in the sky and say a thank-you prayer to her goddess Hathor. In the morning, Kepi and Menes would go to separate spots in the river and strip, and she washed her dress and his *shenti* in the river, rubbing the worst spots with stones. Then they put them on wet and let them dry on their bodies as they paddled. The sun bleached them a nice white every day. It was chilly at first—but it was worth it to be clean again.

When it was too far between towns, they slept onshore in the open. The shoreline was more and more clogged with papyrus reeds, so they had to search for open spots where they could drag the boat out onto the mud. Then Menes would pick a spot to camp, far enough from the water that the crocodiles wouldn't bother them, but close enough that they could dash for the boat if they needed to escape a predator on land. They made huts out of palm fronds—something Kepi had been doing for years with Father, so she was adept at that. And they took turns keeping watch.

On their first night out in the open together, Kepi found a little egg attached to the underside of a milkweed leaf. It was silvery white and shiny, with ribbed sides— so she knew exactly what was in it. She dug up the weed, carefully packing the dirt around the roots, and placed it in the bottom of the boat. She dripped water on the roots every day, and at night she placed the weed beside her as she slept. Sometimes she sang to it, sometimes she just whispered to it.

On the tenth day the egg hatched, and a black-and-white caterpillar with thick yellow spots came out. It had three pairs of long black tentacles. Kepi watched with a proud smile as it proceeded to eat the milkweed plant. It grew fat and even shinier. On the ninth day of being a caterpillar, it changed again and formed a cocoon, all green at first, but it gradually turned to pink over the next week. It hung from the bottom of a leaf of the new milkweed plant Kepi had dug up for it and swung with the rhythm of their paddles. Kepi couldn't wait for the butterfly to come out. It would be soon.

Each day as night came, lions roared in the distance, hyenas made their whooping laughs, jackals howled. Kepi didn't have to pinch herself to stay awake on her watch; she was on edge every second. But there was one thing she did love about sleeping in the open: The mornings were all misty green, as though someone had woven the finest cloth of fresh leaves and draped it over the world. Kepi thought of it as a goddess gown. So she chose early mornings as her time for special talks with the gods. Mostly about all the things she'd seen the day before. Sometimes about her hopes, too. And sometimes about her fears.

A few times they camped at isolated lakes not far in from the river, like the one the pelicans had led them to that first day that Kepi spent on the big trade boat. Menes told her that most of those lakes were formed when the river would shift course, something the Nile did a lot. Others came about after the hot-weather floods, when the river would shrink again and water would get trapped in low spots. Kepi loved the nights at the lakes, because usually the water was too shallow to attract crocodiles, and they were the most peaceful places. Except for that one morning they woke surrounded by a herd of elephants that had come to drink and wallow. Menes had insisted they simply sit still until the beasts left. So Kepi got to watch the young ones' antics.

On the nights at the lakes they ate better, too. The birds were even more plentiful and varied there than on the river. Menes always managed to creep up on ducks or geese and snag one in a net he made himself from the tough fibers of palm fronds. And once they came upon a lone male ostrich. He was small, maybe only a little more than half the height of the ostriches Kepi knew down south, where she came from. He was busy pecking at the remains of a warthog carcass, left behind by lions or a leopard. Menes threw his knife and got the bird right in his skinny neck. He died instantly.

Ostriches were alert birds; no one should have been able to creep up on them—so Kepi was amazed until she saw that this one was missing an eye. So it hadn't been a fair fight, poor ostrich. And ostriches must be sacred to the god Osiris, because he always wore a crown with ox horns and ostrich feathers. Like this ostrich, Osiris was to be pitied. He had been slain by the god Set, and he had to live in the underworld, presiding over the dead, rather than among the living. He might be angry that one of his birds had been so poorly treated. Kepi plucked a glossy black feather from the ostrich and bowed respectfully to it, saying a little prayer of apology to Osiris inside her heart. Then she pushed the feather between two stitches into the hem of her dress. She would treat that one feather reverently till it fell apart.

While Kepi prepared the fire, Menes took care of plucking the bird and cleaning the innards so the bile wouldn't ruin the meat. Despite Kepi's sympathy for the ostrich, she had to admit it was delicious. After that, Kepi stayed on the lookout for more ostriches. But she promised herself that the next time they saw an opportunity for ostrich meat, she'd urge Menes to make sure the bird was strong and healthy before he hunted it.

The voyage was full of marvels. In the quiet times on the river Kepi often thought of Father's words: "If you're searching for a *neter*, a god—observe nature." She had always known that her father was wise, but now she felt his wisdom deep inside her, as though it had entered her very bones.

Thinking about Father like that would make her bottom lip quiver. Her family was so far away, they felt like a dream. And sometimes she had to fight off fears about what might be happening to Babu. And Nanny. But when that happened, she sang. She simply burst out in loud song. And pretty soon Menes joined her. He said she'd caught the spirit of adventure. Maybe he was right.

For going to see the pharaoh was an adventure. He was the most powerful man in the world. This was huge, what she was doing. So huge, Kepi felt it in every stroke of the paddle. She felt it in the sun sparkle on the water and the dew on spiderwebs. She felt it in the call of the monkeys, in the bite of a wild onion's juice, in the heady scent of jasmine. It was behind every prayer. In those moments—the pharaoh moments—she fell silent.

That was when Menes would talk. He'd tell Kepi about places he'd been, things he'd seen, plans he had. It seemed he'd been everywhere and seen everything in all of Egypt. They were becoming friends, really good friends. The only thing they didn't talk about was what was going to happen once they arrived at Ineb Hedj. They both knew their hopes clashed, so why talk about it? But it was good talking about everything else.

Kepi was now deep into the best part of the trip. It had started many days ago, when they first caught a glimpse of the giant pyramid of Djed Snefru rising up out of its enclosing walls. It seemed like a single huge block of white stone, compared with the red mud brick of the homes and shops. They arrived in the town at sunset, and the white stone looked all rosy and warm. Menes took Kepi right up to the smaller pyramid that nestled at the southern base of the big one. They walked around the east side past the chapel, then looked in at the entrance to the pyramid on the north side. A passage descended down to the sunken burial chamber. Kepi's breath caught in awe.

They could still look back over their shoulders and see that pyramid two days later when they arrived at Tashur, where two more giant limestone pyramids dominated the landscape. One had graceful curved sides. It seemed marvelous to Kepi that three majestic tombs should be within sight of one another. The pharaohs entombed there must be happy. And that was as it should be, for all pharaohs were transformed into gods when they assumed the throne. Kepi understood now why Father spoke so proudly of the pyramids.

From Tashur on they could see the great pyramid ahead, the one that Pharaoh Khufu had been building for years, since before Kepi was born, the one that had stolen Father's foot. It was that high, and it wasn't even finished yet.

Kepi was glad she was Egyptian. She was glad she was learning about the Nile, the heartbeat of her country. She thanked the gods and goddesses every night for keeping her alive to see all these wonderful sights. She told herself every day that this voyage was a good thing for her. She told herself that someday she'd see Mother and Father and Nanu again. She would. But first she'd talk to the pharaoh, to a god on earth. And she'd save her family.

All those thoughts made her happy. But somewhere deep inside her, a sadness was growing. A sense of doubt, as though she knew something but couldn't quite grasp it.

22
SANDSTORM

Kepi and Menes took their places in the little boat and paddled away from the dock of the village they'd slept in last night. It was barely dawn—Kepi's favorite time. She looked straight ahead and up a little. If she was lucky, she would see it happen. There was this briefest moment, just a second really, when the sky changed from pale gray but it wasn't yet blue—an instant of startling white. She had seen it several times since she'd been on this voyage, and it always made her feel that she was glimpsing something very special. She had decided it was the smile of a goddess. She didn't know which goddess, but it was so luxurious, it had to be that. Kepi laughed out loud.

"So? You're in a good mood, huh?" said Menes from his spot behind her. "Let's cross the river and stay as close as we can to the west bank."

"How come?"

"I wouldn't want to see you jump in and swim across the whole Nile."

"What are you talking about?"

"You're pretty wild, you know. More like a little animal than a little tempest sometimes. It's impossible to predict what you'll do at the first sight of the white walls."

Kepi pulled her paddle in and rested it across her thighs, so she could turn her head to Menes. He was clearly teasing her, but she had no idea why. "All right. What's going on?"

He grinned. "The west bank is where Ineb Hedj sits. We'll arrive today."

Kepi let out a whoop of joy.

"Not so loud. You'll scare the crocs."

Kepi dug her paddle in deep and pushed it back with all her strength. Today. They were arriving today. This journey was finally over. She might do what she had to do and be on a boat going back home soon. Maybe even tomorrow.

That talk about going over close to the west bank was just Menes's joke. They paddled to the center and stayed there. That was where the current was strongest; that was where they could travel the fastest with the least effort.

And in that moment, the pink cocoon that Kepi had taken such good care of split, and a wet butterfly struggled out.

"Menes, watch."

They both put down their paddles.

The body was black with white spots. The wings were lion colored.

"See that little pouch on the hind wing?" said Kepi.

"The thick spot, you mean?"

"That shows it's a male. My father taught me all about butterflies. This kind is the most common in all Egypt."

The butterfly stretched his wings out wide to dry them. Then he took off, flying straight and low over the water. Kepi watched, her throat tight with worry. But he made it to land and disappeared among the plants at the water's edge. She clapped. So did Menes.

"Kepi, listen. You're smart. You know you can't get your baboon back."

The words felt like a blow to the chest. "Don't say that."

"The crew will have sold him to a temple, and you'll never get him back from the priests. Besides, people can't keep baboons in their homes. He'll grow big, and if he isn't trained properly, he'll be vicious."

"Don't! Don't say such a thing about Babu!" But Menes was right. Kepi realized she'd reached the same conclusion at some point over this past month. That was the cause of the nugget of sadness inside her. Babu was gone for good. She hung her head.

"Don't be stubborn." Menes leaned toward her. "I've made a decision. When we find the crew, I'll get them to give you a share of whatever they got for the baboon."

"I'd never take anything for Babu. You don't trade away a friend!"

"You infuriate me, you know that?" He slapped the side of the boat. "All right, forget it. We'll talk about it when we get to Ineb Hedj."

"I need to talk now. About something else. The pharaoh."

Menes protruded his lips as though appraising her. "Are you really going to try to see him?"

"He hurt my father. Can you tell me where to find him?"

"What do you mean, he hurt your father?"

"My father was working on his pyramid, on the inner chamber, and a chunk of granite fell on his foot. They had to cut it off. Now he can't farm anymore and everything's so hard. We could lose our land."

"That happens all the time, Kepi. Pharaoh Khufu's been building that pyramid for nearly twenty years, and thousands of men have worked on it. I don't know—maybe a hundred thousand. They get maimed. They die."

Kepi pressed her lips together. Of course that was true.

Lots of men were like Father. "So you understand. I have to tell him."

"He doesn't care."

"He has to care. We're his people."

"Khufu's father and grandfather, they were good rulers. Djoser Netjeriket and Snefru. They had compassion. Khufu doesn't know what compassion is."

"Everyone knows what compassion is."

"Let me tell you something. Khufu used to have a magician who was trying to learn how to bring dead people back to life. So he chose prisoners for the magician to practice on. Understand?" Menes jutted his chin forward. "He'd kill them so the magician could try to make them come alive again. But they never did."

Kepi could hardly speak. She whispered, "That's so terrible. Who told you?"

"It's what people say."

"It couldn't be true. It's against the law."

"And people never break the law? Look who you're talking to, Kepi." Menes covered his mouth for a moment. "Let's paddle. I need to think. You should, too. No more talking till we're almost there."

Kepi's insides were jumbled now. But the wood felt smooth and good in her hands. She put all her energy into paddling. She'd think later, when her heart had calmed.

The Nile widened steadily as the morning gently

warmed. They traveled for hours. The river grew posi-
tively swampy at the edges, clogged with weeds and
rushes and the tallest papyrus Kepi had yet seen. A gentle
wind came from the north, like usual. But beyond that,
there was no motion other than the river's current. The
birds seemed to be asleep late today; even the ducks and
geese were absent. And the only herd of gazelles Kepi
had caught sight of was in the distance, hightailing it
away.

"Do you feel that?" Menes asked.

Kepi flinched. Menes's voice was such a surprise in
this quiet that it came as a rude shock. "Feel what?"

"A cold wind."

She hadn't. But now that he said it, she did notice a
slight chill. "Yes."

"Which way do you think it's coming from?"

"Behind."

"I know that, but which way, east or west?"

"I think east."

"Paddle for the west bank as fast as you can!"

"Why? What's the matter?"

"A sandstorm. Paddle! We have to make it to the
west bank before it hits."

Kepi had never been outdoors in a sandstorm. The
very idea terrified her. At home they all huddled in the
storage cellar when the winds blew.

They paddled as hard as they could. The cold wind came faster now. She looked back over her shoulder. A thick cloud was speeding toward them, all red and gold from dust and sand swirling together. It barreled up the river, spreading out as far as she could see to the east. It stretched upward through the skies so that there was no blue beyond. She let out a yelp and paddled harder, faster, deeper.

"All trade boats take passengers," shouted Menes.

"What?"

"I told you it wasn't allowed. I told you that when I first got you to come on our boat. But I was lying. If something happens to me, beg a ride home on a trade boat and they'll take you in exchange for cleaning fish or gear or whatever."

"Nothing's going to happen to you, Menes."

"In my cloth satchel is the glass bead necklace I bought you at Nekheb. I was going to give it to you when we got to Ineb Hedj. Put it on now. Just in case."

Kepi knew what "just in case" meant. "Stop talking like that. We won't die, Menes."

"Set is the god of storms. And you're his little tempest. He might protect you, but he sure won't protect me."

"I didn't pray to Set for a storm. I promise. I'd never do such a thing."

"I know that. Sometimes the gods just do things, all on their own. But I'll fight. I won't give up. And you're like me—you don't give up. You remember that. Whatever happens."

"Stop it! Really. You'll put that necklace on me when we get to Ineb Hedj."

The clear air turned dark gray in an instant, as though someone had just blown out the wick flames in a bowl of kiki oil. The sand cloud reached so high, it blocked out the sun.

Menes steered them into the middle of the closest rushes. The little boat jerked as it slammed against the plants. Menes threw his paddle into the bottom of the boat and grabbed the pole. He poled them deeper into the rushes, till the boat couldn't move at all. Then he opened his cloth satchel and took out a ball of fabric and stared at Kepi. "I only have one."

That ball was a sand scarf. Kepi knew all about them. You wrapped them around your whole head, to protect your eyes from being scratched blind by the sand and to keep the dust and sand from filling up your nose and mouth and suffocating you. The cloth was thin enough to see through, so you could still breathe, and firm enough so that it could hold itself away from your mouth. A flimsy scarf could get pushed into your throat and choke you. Without the protection of the right scarf, no one could survive a sandstorm. Kepi stared back at Menes.

He turned his back to her and wrapped his head, winding fast. Then he stopped and unwound. He looked at Kepi and took out his knife. "You're right. Everyone knows what compassion is." Menes slit the cloth and handed her half. "If we make it through this, I'll go with you to talk to the pharaoh. Hurry now." He closed his eyes and wound his half around his head. Around and around. So fast his hands were a blur. He was expert at it. When he finished winding, he curled up on his side in the bottom of the boat and hugged himself.

Kepi had better be fast, too. She was holding her half by one end when the wind blew upward and snatched it away, over the tops of the papyrus, lost to sight!

The cloud had become a solid wall, pushing forward with wild winds. Only the gods could save her now. Kepi opened her mouth to pray, but the wind stole her words. It pulled her hair. It tried to rip off her dress.

Kepi pulled her dress off over her head and the wind tore at it, but she held on for dear life this time. She tied the top of it into a knot, so the dress was like a bag now. Then she pulled the bag down over her head and bunched the bottom of it around her neck, clutching it tight with her hands. She curled into the bottom of the boat.

The storm roared. It bellowed. It screamed. It was as

though every wild animal in the whole world cried out in anger at once. The dust and sand scoured Kepi's bare skin raw. She tightened into the smallest ball she could, to protect at least the front of her. Her back and upper shoulder burned savagely. She felt something wet spread from that shoulder down to the well of her neck, then get sucked away by the wind. She was bleeding. She'd be skinned completely if her body stayed out in the open like that.

She got to her knees, fighting against the force of the gale, and hurled herself over the edge of the boat. She couldn't even reach out to catch on to anything, because it took all her strength to hold her dress bunched tight around her neck. She landed in papyrus so thick, it was almost impenetrable. It held her up. She thrashed and kicked and wiggled, and slowly, slowly she worked her way down. Her feet found their way under the cool water. What enormous relief. Then her legs and bottom and finally her shoulders. Papyrus surrounded her. It slapped down on her head from every direction.

The storm raged on. The noise deafened her. Her dress blinded her. The water and papyrus enveloped her. She felt a part of her close off from the world outside. It gathered itself together and sealed away in a secret spot she'd never known she had, deep in the center of her being. Was that her *ka*? Was it preparing to separate from her body? Kepi didn't want to die. *Please. Please.*

She pressed the side of her head against the papyrus plants. She could still feel their pressure. But only barely. She wanted to sleep. The need to doze off was huge. But she had the sickening conviction that if she let herself sleep, she'd never wake.

Aiiii! Something bit her foot. Kepi kicked at it like a maniac. She could barely move, wedged into the reeds like that, but she still kicked until she couldn't anymore. It was all she could do just to hold on to her dress and breathe.

And still the storm raged. It just wouldn't stop. Kepi lost all sense of time. It was as though she'd always been here in this water in these papyrus leaves, and she always would be.

Finally the noise lessened. Did it really? Kepi couldn't be sure of anything. Maybe her ears had truly stopped working. For now she couldn't hear anything. It wasn't like before, when she felt deafened by noise. This was just absence. Nothingness. Did she live still? She moved her tongue around in her dry, dry mouth. Her teeth were still there.

23

GONE

Crack!

Kepi dared to stretch a hand upward. Rain came splashing down in big bold drops. But the wind was gone. Kepi pulled her dress off her head.

She had to blink several times before she could see. The world was red and yellow. Dust and sand covered the papyrus leaves. It covered the river weeds and the rushes and the land beyond. It even sat on the surface of the water. But the downpour was quickly doing its job. The dust on the plants turned to mud and slid off.

The sky lit up with a great jagged line of flame from one side to the other. *Crack!*

Kepi stuffed part of her dress in her mouth so she wouldn't lose it, and she used both hands to turn herself around in the reeds. The little papyrus boat was still behind her, but it was upright now, its nose immersed in the river, as though some giant had lifted the rear of it with a finger.

"Menes!" mumbled Kepi. "Menes, where are you?" She grabbed the rim of the side of the boat and pulled herself to it. She reached under the water and felt inside the bow of the boat. There was nothing there. The boat was entirely empty except for the pole, which had somehow gotten speared through the side, high up near the gunwale. She took her dress out of her mouth and shouted, "Menes! Menes, answer me! Where are you?" Her words were lost in the rain. Even she could barely hear them.

Kepi held her dress with her teeth again and pulled herself, hand over hand, along one side of the boat, as if she were climbing a rope. She yanked and struggled, and finally the papyrus yielded and the bow came up and the boat was righted. It was full of dust and sand and water. But it couldn't sink because of the matted papyrus reeds.

The rain pounded. It made the mud in the boat roil. Kepi hauled herself over the side and fell into the little boat. She stood up shakily. She could hardly see anything, the rain came so hard. She crumpled her dress into a ball and clutched it to her belly. "Menes!" she screamed. "Where are you?" She called and called.

She pulled the pole out of the side of the boat and poked it down under the water, through the reeds. He must have jumped into the reeds as she had. He must still be hiding there. "Menes!" She poked everywhere she could reach. She poked and poked. "Menes!" She screamed till her voice was completely gone. But she kept poking. He had to be here somewhere. Maybe he had gotten caught in the papyrus. But he was breathing. He had to be. Where was he? She poked on and on. Inside her heart she prayed to every god she could think of. *Save him. Save Menes. Don't let his body be lost in the river. Don't let his* ka *be alone forever. Save him. Please. One of you, please please, save him.*

The rain gradually came to a halt. The sun glowed far in the west. It was late afternoon. A crocodile silently glided by on the river behind Kepi. Ducks quacked. The air came to life again.

"Menes," Kepi whispered. She put her face into the reeds and drank. "Menes," she said, louder now. Her voice had returned. "Menes!" she shouted. And she went back to poking. "Menes! Don't do this! Don't be gone. Please, Menes."

The crocodile glided past again with egg-yolk-yellow eyes.

"Is that you, great god Sobek? Don't just glide on past. If that's you, help me. Please help me."

The crocodile blinked several times, then went under without a sound.

Ke-ke-ke-pi. A thin cry came from overhead. It was a vulture.

"Great goddess Nekhbet?" Kepi called. "You protect the pharaoh. But we're the pharaoh's people. Please protect us."

Kepi watched the vulture till it glided out of sight. Not once did it flap its wings.

There was no one else around, no one else to appeal to. The day was passing. This little boat couldn't stay on the water in the dark.

Kepi made a bowl of her hands and slowly scooped the mud from inside the boat. Then she used the pole to push the boat out of the papyrus reeds. Once it was free, she leaned over the side and dipped her dress in the water to rinse it of the mud. Then she put it on, sopping wet.

And all the while, tears rolled down her cheeks. But she didn't think about why. She didn't really think at all. Her body just did things on its own.

She had no paddle. Nothing but the pole. She used the pole to push the boat out until it was too deep to reach the bottom anymore. Then she sat and waited. The current took the boat, slowly at first, then faster, to the middle of the river. She had no way to steer, no way to increase or decrease her speed. She just went with the river, and the river went fast. The rain had dropped so much water that the current was stronger than Kepi had ever felt it.

After a long time, she passed an overturned boat. A big one of wood planks. Broken into pieces and half sunk. But she was pretty sure it wasn't the trade boat that had carried her Babu.

She passed a floating body—a woman. She looked away.

It was early evening when she saw the white walls. They went on forever. Pure white stone walls, still wet from the rains that had followed the sandstorm. The dying light of day glistened orange off the tiny puddles that formed in the crevices. And the buildings within those walls, oh! There were so many. Kepi had never imagined that a city could bring together so many people. Date palms grew in clusters within the walls. The dock was littered with broken boats. Children carried debris from the storm down to the river and dumped it in. A boy looked up and saw her and waved.

That was when Kepi realized she was going to drift on by the city. She had no way of getting to shore. "Help!" she shouted. "I have no paddle. Help!"

The boy just waved.

"Help!" Kepi stood, her legs wide to brace against the movement of the boat. She held up the pole. "This is all I have. Help me get to shore! Help!"

By this point a few of the children had gathered to watch her. They talked with one another. One of them went running back into the city. He must be going for help. But Kepi was floating on by. She couldn't wait or she'd be lost. Again. She wouldn't let that happen, never again.

She dove into the river and swam for the dock. It was far and the river was strong, but Kepi was stronger. This month of constant paddling had transformed her. Her arms were hard as those stone walls. If a crocodile came up to her, she'd punch him in the nose.

The children on the dock shouted now. They jumped and urged her on. "Swim! Swim fast!"

And she did. Kepi, who had never been a good swimmer, who had lagged behind Nanu in every race—Kepi swam as though the water was her home. She reached the dock, and many hands pulled her up.

"What happened?"

"Why were you out on the river?"

"You weren't on the river during the storm, were you?"

"No one could survive the sandstorm on the river. My father said so."

"Mine, too."

"Why were you all alone?"

Kepi shook her head and dropped to the ground. "I

wasn't all alone. I wasn't. But he's gone." And her tears came again, this time with knowledge. She cried for Menes. For Menes, who had lied to her and stolen her and wanted to sell her. For Menes, who had fed her and protected her and taught her and shared his sand cloth with her. He shouldn't have died. No no no. She beat her chest in grief.

Two men came out on the dock carrying a papyrus boat.

"She's safe," one of the boys called to them. "She swam to shore. She swam among the crocodiles. The gods protected her."

"Where's the boat?"

The boy pointed. Kepi's little boat was far down the river now.

The men put their boat in the water and paddled fast. Kepi watched as they reached her boat. She watched as one of them climbed into it and both of them paddled the two boats back to the dock.

The man in Kepi's boat jumped out and pulled on the boat.

"I'll take one side," said Kepi. And she helped him haul it onto the dock.

"It's ours now," said the man to Kepi. "You abandoned it. It's ours." He pointed at the two tallest boys. "Help us carry these boats away."

The rest of the boys left, too. Only the boy who had first waved at Kepi remained. "Go home," he said. But nicely.

"I don't have a home. Not in Ineb Hedj."

"So what are you doing here?"

"I don't know. I used to know. But right now I can't . . . I can't think. I'm just sad."

"I know. I saw you cry."

Kepi shivered. She shivered and shivered, uncontrollably. "Can I stay with you tonight?"

The boy didn't even blink. "You're strong. You can do boys' work. I'm Masud. Come, and you can stay as long as you like."

24

METALLURGY

The master came and stood on the other side of Masud. Kepi sensed Masud stiffening. But she kept her eyes steady on the hole in front of them.

The master gave a quick nod. "Line it." He hobbled off to inspect the work of the boys at the other fire pits.

Masud smiled at Kepi. "He's pleased. We dug it the right size."

Kepi could take no credit. Masud was the one who knew about these things; Kepi had never dug a fire pit before. She sighed and looked around.

At that moment, a vulture landed on the gate of the metallurgy yard. Two people were peering through that gate into the yard: a boy of around eight years old and a man sitting on a mat of papyrus reeds woven together. The boy held one end of a rope. The other end was tied to the mat. The man's legs were stumps. Boy and man were both hollow eyed and hollow cheeked. A dullness sat on their open lips.

"We're being watched," said Kepi.

"Don't look at them. If the master sees, he'll chase them off before they've had a chance."

"A chance at what?"

"Don't talk."

Masud looked around quickly. With his back to the gate, he tossed a pottery shard over his shoulder. The vulture didn't move, though the shard went right past him and landed beyond the boy. The boy picked it up and left, pulling the man on the mat behind him.

And the whole time Masud hadn't even glanced at them. He was already on his knobby knees, lining the bottom and the sides of the hole with the pottery shards. So Kepi did the same. For the past three days, ever since she'd met Masud on the dock and come here to this metallurgy shop, she'd mimicked everything he did, never asking questions. Masud said it was best not to call attention to oneself. People who stuck out got beaten or given more work.

Mimicking was fine with Kepi. Last night was the first time she'd really slept since the sandstorm. Since Menes had died. So she'd been tired most of the time. She didn't have the energy to think for herself. She was grateful to drift along at this quiet shop; no one drowned here, no one starved. It was easy to lose herself in the strange details of this new life. She was grateful for that, too.

Today, though, Kepi was rested, and her thinking was sharp again. She didn't fully understand what had happened just now with that boy and the man outside the gate, but she knew they were homeless. Beggars. Masud had somehow helped them by giving them something as worthless as a pottery shard. He would get in trouble if the master knew. And he trusted Kepi not to tell on him.

And most of all, something had happened to that man's legs.

For the first time in three days, Kepi felt something beyond grief. She was startled to find that it was almost disgust—at herself. She'd been hardly a person; it was as though she had no will of her own. She'd let herself act helpless.

Father always said the only thing that was humiliating was helplessness. Kepi suddenly realized that that belief probably made the loss of his foot that much more difficult for him. And it was part of what made him so determined to be not just a baker, but the best baker around. He wouldn't give up. And Menes was like Father—not in most ways, but in that one way. When the crew stole Babu and made off without him, he didn't cry—he got mad. He said, "No one gets away with stealing from me."

Kepi was sick of herself. Menes had called Kepi his

stubborn little tempest, but it was Menes who was stubborn. And so was Father. No one ever called her father stubborn, but now it was obvious to Kepi that that was exactly what Father was. You had to be stubborn when things got awful, or you'd give up. And giving up felt awful. Menes had told her to remember that, remember never to give up.

Kepi loved Father. And she had come to love Menes. She would probably never stop feeling a heavy sadness for Menes, but she could carry it around with more strength if she did what she knew she really should be doing. For the love of both her family and Menes, she had to find that stubborn core within again and gain the strength from it to shake herself into action.

Because this whole thing had grown. It was clear to Kepi now; like dawn after a long night out in the open by the river, everything was clear. Lots of people got hurt working on the pyramids. So it wasn't just her family that depended on her. In a way, all Egypt depended on her, because all Egypt depended on the pharaoh. And Kepi loved Egypt. Her month alone with Menes on the river had made that love deep and abiding. This was her land. Kepi needed to tell the pharaoh about all of them, all the injured workers. Maybe that was why the vulture had drawn her attention to that boy and man on the other side of the gate; maybe it was the goddess

Nekhbet, the goddess who protected the pharaoh. She had soared overhead after the sandstorm, and now she had come again. Maybe she wanted Kepi to talk with the pharaoh and help him change his ways, help him become a better god.

It all made sense, this whole trip. A fierce determination flowed through her. But Kepi shouldn't do anything fast. For the moment she had to do her job, or both she and Masud would get in trouble. And Masud was really nice; Kepi never wanted to get him in trouble. Tonight, while everyone else was sleeping, she'd figure out what to do next. She looked around through newly alert eyes. Metallurgy was interesting; she might as well pay attention.

Masud now dumped charcoal into the hole. He lit a papyrus torch from one of the other boys' fires and set the charcoal aflame. He sucked his top lip in behind his bottom teeth. Kepi had seen him do that a lot.

"What's the matter?" she asked. Why wasn't he gathering the green rocks and throwing them into the fire pit? That was the next step. That was what they'd done for the past three days. Those rocks contained copper, and copper was what they were smelting.

Kepi had known how to recognize copper since she was tiny. Back home those blue-green nuggets lay near streams. Once, after a thunderstorm, Kepi and Father had gone wandering in a canyon and had come across a large cliff hunk that had fallen off. Red speckled the broken side. Father told her that was the original color of copper—before the wind and rain turned it green. Brilliant red. And that was how it looked here, after they smelted it and the master made it into bracelets and anklets.

When Masud didn't answer, Kepi nudged him. "Are you daydreaming?" She pointed at the rock pile. "Let's go get them."

"Don't point," said Masud under his breath. "And don't look at me when you talk. The master doesn't like us to talk at work. And no, of course I'm not daydreaming. Don't treat me like a silly jackass."

That was one of Masud's favorite insults: He called the other boys silly jackasses. Jackasses were four-legged animals with short hair that stood as tall as Kepi and had hooves that weren't split. They stank, although Masud insisted they smelled nice after a bath. In Kepi's opinion, the people in Ineb Hedj didn't wash their jackasses often enough. In Upper Egypt, where Kepi was from, they didn't have jackasses. But this city was crowded with them. The millers used them to stomp grains into flour. And everyone used them to carry burdens. Kepi didn't know if jackasses were silly or not, but she liked the insult because it made her feel just the slightest bit as though she was home, with Father and Mother and Nanu calling her silly all the time.

"So what's the matter?" Kepi asked out of the side of her mouth.

"We're doing something different today. Just you and me. The master chose us. Well, he chose me—he always chooses me for special tasks; but I asked for you as my partner. That's why we dug this new pit." Masud rubbed his nose and talked with his hand in front of his mouth. "And it's my first time. We have to do it right. Don't ask questions. Just do what I do." He put charcoal into a pot about a quarter of the way full and set it beside the flaming pit. Kepi was baffled, but Masud clearly wasn't about to offer an explanation.

Masud picked up two metal rods and handed one to Kepi. Together they went to their old fire pit from yesterday, the one that was completely cool now. The rocks they'd melted in that pit had resolidified into a single big slab. They used the metal rods to dig out the slab and levered it onto the ground beside the pit. Then Masud cracked the rod down on top of it. "Come on," he said. "This is the fun part. Try it."

So they took turns hitting the slab. A brittle, glassy, silvery layer chipped off. "That's slag," said Masud. "The junk rock that the copper ran through." Underneath was the beautiful, glistening, pure red copper. Masud brushed it off with his hands. "Help me carry it to our new pit."

Kepi was surprised. Usually the master had the cakes of pure copper carried to his workshop. There boys hammered them so flat that the master could cut and bend them any way he wanted. Jewelry, bowls, boxes, mirrors. Sometimes the master set colored stones into box lids—amethyst, carnelian, quartz, garnet. Kepi loved the mirrors especially, because the master outlined them with bits of turquoise, the color that ensured fertility and protected against the evil eye. Kepi wanted a copper mirror with a turquoise border when she got older. Nanu would love one now.

So it was odd to carry the copper cake to the new flaming pit. But Kepi obediently curled her fingers under her end of the slab.

The fire glowed blue already.

"I'm a silly jackass," said Masud. "We should have put the pot of charcoal in the pit when the flames were still red. Now the fire's so hot, we'll get burned."

"We have to put the pot in the fire pit?"

"I told you not to ask questions."

Kepi looked at the pot. It had a lip around the top. "If we hold the metal rods under the lip, you on one side and me on the other, we can lift it in without getting burned. It'll be easy because we're just about the same height."

Masud knitted his brows. "Please, great god Seker," he said softly. "Please help us. Don't let us drop the pot. You love jewelry, and we are metalworkers, so we are your humble servants."

Kepi and Masud used the rods to place the pot in the fire. Then Masud set the charcoal inside the pot afire. "Now the copper cake goes in."

Kepi blinked. "How? There's no way to hold it at a distance, and we can't throw it in or the pot will break."

Masud didn't even look at Kepi. He picked up a stone and hammered the tip of a rod into one end of the thin slab. Slowly the rod pierced the copper cake. He smiled at her triumphantly. "See, you're not the only smart one. Pure copper is soft." They skewered the copper slab and lifted it down into the pot, then slid out the rod.

Masud pumped air into the side of the pit with a goatskin bellows. The fire grew white hot. Then Masud tossed a dark, shiny, silvery rock into the molten copper.

Kepi stepped back in alarm. "You're dirtying the copper again."

"It's *upje*. That's what we're supposed to do."

"I never heard of *upje*."

"Some call it arsenic. It makes bronze. A harder

metal. Better for statues."

"Statues? Are we making statues?"

"Not us. Just watch."

Stinking fumes rose from the molten soup—like old, wet, musty garlic that had grown extra strong.

The master looked into their pot. Then he called over the dozen other boys to sit in a semicircle and watch. But Masud and Kepi were told to stay on their feet, so they could see everything better.

Kepi didn't like standing when everyone else was sitting. She could tell from their faces that it made the boys angry. Masud and she were the only free people working here. The other children were slaves, stolen or traded for from other countries.

Masud was an orphan. The master had adopted him. But he showed the boy no affection. Masud said that the master had adopted him only because he wanted to make sure he'd have someone to take care of him in his old age. So Masud was learning the trade—the master taught him everything, not just the menial tasks. When the other boys got older, the master would trade them away and get younger slaves, but Masud would stay here his whole life.

Masud had told the master that Kepi was an orphan, too. He hadn't lied, though. That was what he had believed when he'd first brought her to the workshop.

Now he knew all about her, but he hadn't then.

The master took long metal tongs, and with great effort, he lifted the pot from the fire pit and set it on the ground. He was a big man, but he was lame in one leg, so everything was hard for him. He hammered a hole in the side of the pot, up near the top.

Kepi noticed that a slave boy was trying to peer past her. It was the odd slave boy—the one the others kept their distance from, as though there was something wrong with him. He was tall, but she was exactly in his way. Their eyes met. She moved aside so he could see.

Now the master gripped the pot with the tongs and tipped it. Molten metal poured through that hole into a casting mold. The rising steam made it hard to see, but as it cleared, a golden thread appeared, connecting the pot to the mold. It seemed sublime, like the long shiny finger of a god.

The master threw the empty pot onto the shard pile. Then he squatted by the casting mold. After a long while, he tapped the mold with a hammer, and it broke away from what was inside.

Two golden ears appeared, pointing to the heavens. Then a head with deeply incised long whiskers. The cat sat on its haunches with its tail straight up. The master rubbed with a thick cloth until the cat glowed. At last he held it up for all to see. "I made this for rich customers," said the master. "Do you think they'll like it?"

The slave boys cheered.

It was afternoon by now. The fires in the other pits had died down. The master told the boys to put away the tools; they were free till dinnertime.

"I have an errand," Masud said to Kepi. "Want to come?"

Kepi hadn't yet been out of this shop, except to go back and forth to the home they ate and slept in. The offer tempted her. But her curiosity was piqued even more about something else right now. She shook her head, and Masud left.

25
BELLS

Kepi went to the wall of the workshop and sat in the shadows to wait. She was familiar enough with cats; wild cats stalked the refuse pile outside her village. But she wondered who on earth would commission a statue of a cat, of all things.

Soon enough, Kepi heard musical clinks; these customers clearly wore lots of jewelry. Kepi heard the master meet them at the entrance and lead them inside. She stood and peeked in through a window.

A couple with long, drawn faces and many bracelets, anklets, and necklaces followed the master. Their eyebrows were shaved. At the sight of the cat statue, they gasped. "It makes us think of our dear departed one." The woman beat her chest in grief, as though the cat was a member of her family. The man paid and carried away the statue.

Kepi backed into the shadows again and plopped down, almost landing on the lap of one of the slave boys.

"Sorry. I didn't see you." It was the boy she had moved aside for earlier. "I saw the customers," she said in a confidential tone. "That statue is for their dead cat. Imagine that! They owned a wild cat."

"It probably wasn't really wild. It's popular here to tame cats. When one is really nice, they mate it with another really nice one, and the kittens are even nicer. They sleep with them."

"You're joking. Cats in a house?"

"Cats keep poisonous snakes out. And rats, too. People say they're wonderful. I bet the owners shaved their eyebrows."

"They did!" said Kepi.

"I told you. It's what they do here to show respect at the death of a cat."

"How do you know so much about Ineb Hedj?"

"I've lived here since I was six. Half my life."

Kepi swallowed. Half his life away from his family. "I'm Kepi."

"You probably don't want to talk with me, Kepi."

"Why not?"

"I was a swineherd before I came here. The master says swineherds stink. He says that's why I'm bad. He beats me. If he sees us talking, he might beat you, too."

Kepi worked to keep her face placid. Her family said swineherds stank, too. She took a deep breath without being obvious about it. This boy didn't stink. And it wasn't his fault that his family kept swine. "I don't care. I'm happy to know you."

The boy stared. Then he gave a quick head bow. "Call me Kan. But that's not really my name. I was born in Kanesh, so that's what the man who bought me from my parents called me for short, and it stuck."

His parents traded him away! Kepi looked down at her feet so Kan couldn't see the shock in her eyes. In Egypt no one would do that to their children. "Kanesh. Where is that place?"

"Northeast. In the land of the Hattians. It takes months on the backs of jackasses to get there."

"My home is far, too. But south. It takes a month and a half to get there by boat."

"My home has mountains all around," said Kan. Then he gave a little *humph*. "Actually, I don't remember it that well. Sometimes I think I don't remember it at all."

"I remember home. I haven't been away so long, though—not even two months. I think about it all the time. I think about my mother and father and my sister Nanu." Talking like this made Kepi tremble.

"Yeah." Kan looked away. "At least we're busy here. You won't be able to think about them so much as long as you're working the metals."

"I'm not working here long. I only came by accident,

really. It all started because of a baboon."

"Baboon? You mean a monkey?"

Kepi hadn't meant to talk about Babu. She'd given up hope of ever seeing him again. But it felt nice to remember him right now. "The best little monkey."

Kan gave a twisted smile. "Is that a joke?"

"Two boys stole him, and I went after them to get him back. Anyway, he's lost. But I have something else I need to do now. Then I'm going home."

"Sure." Kan laughed. "Just like I'm going home."

"Don't laugh. I'm going to do it." Kepi got to her feet. Beyond the wall of the metallurgy yard, she could see, the sky was decorated with upward swirls of pale-gray smoke from cooking fires. So many of them. So many people were preparing their evening meals.

She looked into the window of the workshop again. The master had left. The workbenches were covered with jewelry in various stages of completion. She thought of the glass bead necklace Menes had bought her in Nekheb, the one she'd never seen. She wished she had let him give it to her then, so that now she'd have a token of him. "I miss jewelry," said Kepi. "I used to wear so much that I jangled wherever I went."

Kan jumped to his feet as though a scorpion had pinched his bottom. "I have something to show you, then." He took off the little pouch that hung around his neck and shook the contents into his hand. Several tiny silvery-white metal bowls, each no bigger than a fingertip, lay in his palm. They each had a miniature loop on the underside of the bowl basin.

"Can I touch them?"

"Sure."

Kepi held two up to the late afternoon sun. "I've never seen anything like this. Are they made of a special silver?"

"It's tin. In my country we smelt it out of rocks, just like we smelt copper here. The man who first owned me had a whole sack of pure tin pebbles, and I stole some before he traded me away. It's all I have left of my country. I made these from a tin pebble."

"What are they for?"

He flipped each basin over so the loops stuck out on top. "They're bells."

"What are bells?"

"Listen." Kan put the rest of the bells away in his pouch. Then he pulled a thread from the edge of his loincloth and ripped it in half with his teeth. He strung the thread through the loops on the two bells and shook. The bells hit each other and gave off the sweetest high-pitched tinkling sound.

"Marvelous," whispered Kepi. Her whole body had tensed up. The tinkle of those bells felt familiar. They sounded like the noise Kepi had imagined the goddess Hathor's necklace must make. That tinkle was more beautiful than the best music she'd ever heard. It filled her with joy. "Bells are completely marvelous."

"When I hear them, it makes me think I remember being small and happy, and maybe someday I'll be happy like that again." Kan put the tin bells back into the pouch and looked at her with a serious face. "Come on. Let's take another tin pebble and make more bells. For you."

Breathless, Kepi waited in the workshop while Kan went to get a tin pebble from his hiding place. They hammered the tin flat enough to break into two pieces; then each of them hammered their piece even flatter. It was soft and gave way easily. But it still took Kepi a long time to make it thin enough for bells as delicate as the ones Kan had in his pouch.

"Hear that?" Kan held a piece of tin close to Kepi's ear and folded it. It gave off the strangest crackle. "It's crying. You have to be gentle, because tin feels everything." He showed Kepi how to fold tin the right way, so that each bell would have a loop at the top for stringing.

It was tricky and took all of Kepi's attention. In the end, she made five tin bells. The evening light had grown dim. Kan handed her a thread, and Kepi strung the bells together and shook them. They tinkled perfectly. How amazing that Kepi had made them so fine when her hands moved so clumsily at the task. They were as wonderful as jewelry. They made her feel like the old Kepi, the one who had a family that gave her jewelry. And the music these bells made was even better than the music jewelry made. The music made her feel she belonged to the goddess Hathor. It made her believe that Hathor was watching her. Of course! Hathor must have helped her make them. Hathor must have guided her clumsy hands. Hathor wanted her to have these bells. *Thank you, great goddess Hathor. Thank you, thank you.*

"You're a tinker now," said Kan. "Anyone who makes things from tin is a tinker. Make sure you never take them out in snow, or they'll turn to gray powder."

"I've never seen snow," said Kepi, holding the precious bells to her chest. She wouldn't even know what snow was if Father hadn't told her about it.

"I was just teasing. We have snow in my country. Seriously, though, never let them fall into a fire, or they'll break."

"I won't," said Kepi, holding them closer.

"If you polish those bells, they'll shine as bright as silver. Now look at what I made." Kan held the thing he'd been working on to his mouth and blew. It gave off a loud, shrill sound.

Kepi jumped in surprise.

"It's a whistle. A boy from my country was here a

couple of years ago. He taught me how to make them before he was traded away again. Isn't it great?"

"Indeed!" The master came into the workshop through the gloom of early evening. "What do you have there, boy?"

Kan put the whistle behind his back. "Nothing."

"It doesn't sound like nothing."

"It's mine."

The master scowled. "What's yours is mine. You belong to me, you dirty little pig herder. You'll get a beating for talking back, all right. And you . . ." He looked at Kepi. "What have you got?"

"We made them," said Kepi, moving to stand beside Kan. "They're ours."

"Anything made in my workshop is mine." The master held out his hands, one toward Kan and one toward Kepi.

Kepi's fingers closed tight on the bells. She'd never give them up. She saw the skin on Kan's jaw tighten as he clenched his teeth.

Kan and Kepi looked at each other, and almost as if they'd known all along this had to happen, they ran together out of the workshop, out of the metallurgy yard, out into the streets of Ineb Hedj.

26
MASUD

"Kepi! Kepi, are you here?" came the raspy call. Kepi opened her eyes. It was the middle of the night, but the moon was bright. She didn't dare move quickly, or the boat might rock and give her away. Kan lay sleeping beside her. They had taken refuge on a small fishing boat at the docks. Kan knew the way, because the slave boys often carried the garbage down here to dump into the river.

Now Kepi slowly closed her fingers around the handle of the paddle beside her. If that call came from the master and if he tried to do anything horrible, she would swing it hard at him. He was big—but that lame leg made him slow. Maybe a blow with the paddle could hold him off long enough to get away.

"Kepi, come on. You have to be here. Don't act like one of the jackass boys!"

Kepi sat up. "Masud?" she hissed.

"There you are." Masud ran along the docks and

stood in front of their boat. "I saved you bread from the evening meal."

Kan jumped up at Masud's voice. He rubbed his eyes. "Bread? Where is it?"

Masud held out two small pieces. "It's not much. Sorry."

Kan climbed from the boat onto the dock and took a piece of the bread.

Kepi carefully felt in the bottom of the boat and found the five tin bells she'd made. She closed them in her fist, climbed out, and took the bread. "Thank you, Masud."

Masud squatted. "Get down like me. That way if anyone should look toward the dock, they're less likely to see us."

Kan and Kepi squatted.

"How did you find us?" asked Kepi.

"I figured the dock was the only place in the city you knew other than the metallurgy shop and the workers' home. Besides, you lived on a boat for so long." He watched them chew the bread.

Kepi could see from his face that he was hungry, too. He had saved these pieces from his own meal, and Kepi knew how skimpy the workers' meals were. She swallowed the last bite gratefully. Then she searched with her fingers for that loose spot in her dress hem. She carefully pushed in the tiny tin bells, one by one, and worked them around to the side, where the ostrich feather nestled.

"When the master told us you'd stolen things and run away, he said you'd either die of starvation or come back like begging dogs."

"We didn't steal," said Kan quickly.

"I know. I came looking for Kepi when I got back from an errand, and I saw the two of you through the rear window in the workshop. I was about to come in when the master caught you. He's a big liar jackass. You won't come back, will you?"

Kepi shook her head. "I'm going home."

"That's good."

"Only I'm going to do what I came here for first."

"I knew you'd try." He pressed a fist against his mouth. Then he spoke slowly. "I've thought and thought about this. And not just tonight. I've been thinking about it ever since . . ." Masud looked at Kepi. "Ever since I met you." He took a deep breath and let it out loudly. "I'll help you. Because I'm free, I get to walk all over. And I was born here—I've been here all my life—so I know this city. I can find out things. You need me. And . . ." He hesitated. ". . . I'll go with you. To your home. I'll help you get there, and then . . . I'll become a metallurgist in your village. There's nothing left here for me now."

Kan groaned. "Kepi told me her plans last night. I

didn't believe her, but it's really going to happen. You're both going to leave." He crossed his arms at the chest and rubbed his forearms. He curled forward even more against his knees, as if he was cold. "What have I done? Oh, I've been so stupid!" he muttered with his head down. "The master will hate me even more now, and I have no place else to go. I'll starve"

"Come with us," said Masud. "You can work with me when we get to Kepi's village."

"Do you really mean that?"

"You're good at metallurgy."

Kan's forehead crinkled, and for a moment Kepi thought he might do something awful—shout or cry, she couldn't tell which. "So, what do we do now?" he asked softly.

"Good," said Kepi. She turned to Masud. "I'll talk to the pharaoh. Then we can beg a ride on a trade boat and leave this place fast."

"It won't be that easy." Masud sucked his top lip behind his bottom teeth. "The pharaoh won't talk to you."

"What do you mean? I'll just go up to him and—"

"He doesn't give private audiences to anyone unless they're the head priest of a town or an ambassador from another land. I asked around. Petitioners have to be important, Kepi. He'd never talk to a kid like you."

"Then I'll jump out at him as he's walking down the street."

"You can't get near him. He's surrounded by servants and dignitaries."

"No!" wailed Kepi.

"There is one chance. Sometimes he gives a public audience. I don't know when the next one is. Or where. But I can find out and get directions. Ineb Hedj is big."

"It can't be that big," said Kepi. "We can—"

"Thirty thousand people. It's the biggest city in the world."

Thirty thousand. The number was staggering. "All right. Let's start asking."

"No," said Masud. "I have to do it. Alone."

Kepi pushed him in the shoulder. "This is my job."

"And you're wanted. The master went to the authorities after the evening meal and told them you stole his slave and the two of you stole his goods. You both have to hide while I find out everything."

"They're looking for us." Kan's fingers dug into his arms now. His skin seemed to turn pale gray in the moonlight. "We're done for."

"No, you're not. I have a place to hide you."

"What about you?" asked Kepi. "Where will you be?"

"I have to stay at the metallurgist's. The master knows I'm your friend. If I leave, he'll tell lies about me, too. The only way I can be free to walk around and ask questions is if I go on working. The master sends me on errands often, so I can ask then. And in the evenings after the meal, I can ask around, too. It's the only way. I've thought it through—it's all I've been thinking about. This is how it has to be." Masud stood. "Come."

Kepi started to rise, but Kan caught her by the elbow. "Wait. The master favors you, Masud. You're his adopted son. How do we know you're not working for him?"

Masud bent over them and opened his hands wide. "You have to trust me."

Kepi thought of how Masud had thrown the pottery shard to the boy and the legless man on the other side of the metallurgy yard gate. "I do trust you," she said, "but I don't understand you. Why would you do all this just for me?"

"It isn't just for you. My mother died when I was born. So it was only my father and me." Masud took a deep noisy breath. "He died working on the pharaoh's pyramid."

Kepi's nose prickled from held-back sobs. "I'm sorry, Masud."

"Follow me."

"Where are you leading us?" asked Kan.

"To a pottery workers' home. My cousin lives there. Our fathers died together—and when I went to the metallurgist, she went to the potter."

"Does the master know about your cousin?" asked Kan.

"Yes," said Masud. "Oh. Oh, you're right, I'm not good at this." He sank back to a squat and dropped his head into his hands. "I don't know anyone else we can trust."

Kan suddenly clapped his hands. "Yes, you do. Amisi."

Masud's jaw dropped. "Right! Amisi lives in the weavers' home."

Amisi meant "flower." It was the sort of name any girl would love to have. Kepi had been among only men or boys for so long, she felt strange at the very thought of another girl. "Who's Amisi?"

"An orphan who was brought to the metallurgist last year," said Masud. "Amisi didn't last; the work was too hard."

"And the master treated her too mean," said Kan.

"Why? What's wrong with her?"

"Her father was an embalmer," said Masud.

Embalmers were outcasts.

"But don't pass judgment on her," said Kan. "Amisi's as close to perfect as a girl gets."

Kepi wasn't about to pass judgment on Amisi. But she

didn't like the way Kan talked about Amisi. "What's so perfect about her?"

"Wait till you see her," said Masud.

Now Masud was doing it, too. Kepi wanted to pinch them both.

"Do you know where the weavers' home is?" asked Kan.

"Stay close. Let's go."

27
HIDING PLACE

Kan stopped in the middle of the road. "Is the weavers' home far from our metallurgy shop?"

"Not very."

"Then we have to pass by there first," said Kan. "I need to get something."

Masud slapped his head in disbelief. "Do you have fever in your heart, so you can't act sensible? You can't go anywhere near there."

"You can, though. And everyone's still asleep. So no one will see you. But if anyone does, you'll think of some excuse."

Masud shook his head hard. "It's too dangerous. I'll bring you to Amisi now. And I'll find an excuse to go on an errand when daylight comes, and I'll bring you what you want then."

"I have to have it now." Kan's voice was hard as stone. "Now!"

"All right." Masud put his hand on Kan's shoulder.

"All right, all right. So, Kan, tell me where these tin pebbles are."

"How did you know I was talking about tin pebbles?"

Masud shrugged sheepishly and turned his face away. "I guess I was listening to you and Kepi in the workshop for a little longer than I said."

Something about his tone calmed Kepi's heart. It was affectionate. She didn't think she'd mind meeting Amisi, after all.

"You know the big white rock by the wall in the outside work area? The one shaped like a giant turtle?" said Kan.

"Near the latrine?"

"Under that rock is a hole. My bag of tin nuggets is there."

"Right near the latrine?" said Masud again. "What a disgusting place to hide something."

"Exactly. No one hangs around the latrine any longer than they have to. No one would look there."

Masud blew through his lips and made a blubbery sound. Kepi's heart jumped. That's what she always used to do to annoy Nanu.

"All right," said Masud. "Let's go."

They raced through the maze of streets of the sleeping city, each one holding on to the elbow of the one in front, Masud in the lead. Some streets were so narrow, moonlight couldn't enter. They ran through solid black. Kepi clutched Kan's elbow with all her might.

The night street sweepers hadn't made it yet to many of the streets they traveled. Kepi felt squishy things underfoot. The sharp, sour smell of jackass dung hung in the air.

She slammed into Kan's back. The boys had stopped.

"Wait here," whispered Masud. "I'll sneak to the latrine. If anyone catches me, I'll say I had a stomach-ache, and I'll go to my sleeping mat. It'll be too risky for me to do anything else."

"But then what'll we do?" asked Kepi.

"If I don't come back by dawn, hide. You'll find some-place. Then meet me here, right at this spot, after the evening meal." Masud cleared his throat. "Or we could go back to my original plan. Do you really need that tin right now, Kan?"

"Yes."

Kan was stubborn, but Kepi remembered how he had talked about the tin, how it was the only thing he still owned from his country. She interlaced her fingers and pressed them against her mouth.

Masud left.

Kepi and Kan squatted by a wall. They heard an animal stomp on the other side, probably in its sleep. Something small crawled on Kepi. She swatted it away and moved closer to Kan. A nightjar swooped down and caught something in midair and glided off.

Oh, dear. Nightjars were active in the evening and at dawn—but not in the middle of the night. Was the air beginning to lighten? It seemed more gray now than black. Something clunked. The people in this house must be waking up. Where could they hide?

Footsteps came running toward them. Kepi jumped up to run the other way.

Kan caught her. "It's Masud."

Kepi's knees went weak with relief. She pressed against the wall to keep from sinking.

Masud handed Kan a bag. Instant energy zapped through all three of them. They ran, without a word, turning this way and that. Noises of people and animals stirring came from every direction.

Masud finally stopped. "That's the weavers' home. I have to get back fast. I'll find you here tonight. I promise. Pray to the goddess Nit for help."

"Why Nit?" asked Kan.

"She's the goddess who protects weavers. Kepi's going to be a weaver now. And you'll hide in the weavers' home—so you'd better pray she protects you, too." And he left.

"Let's pray," said Kepi.

Kan shook his head. "I don't share your gods. I'll pray to my own."

Dear, dear Nit, Kepi prayed inside her heart. *Remember me? You sent the click beetle that led me to Babu. I took good care of your beetle. And I took good care of Babu until he was stolen. I whispered to you from inside the basket when we docked at your favorite city, Ta-senet. Please remember me. Please take care of me. And of Kan, too. He doesn't know our prayers—he doesn't know our gods. But he's a good person.* Then Kepi remembered it was safest with the gods to ask for something specific, to pray that no one would get hurt. *Please don't let the authorities find us in the weavers' home. And please let the pharaoh give a public audience soon.*

"Are you done?" asked Kan. Kepi nodded. "Come on, then." He went right up to a window and looked inside. Then he climbed in.

"What are you doing?" Kepi's heart beat so fast, she panted. "You can't just go through a window like a thief."

"Do you have a better idea?" Kan reached out an arm. "Come on. I'll help you."

"I don't need help." Kepi looked up and down the alley. She couldn't see anyone watching. She climbed in.

The room was empty, and Kan had already opened a door on the other side of it. Kepi ran to stand behind him.

"Look." Kan jerked his chin toward the room. "She's got to be in there."

The room was full of sleeping girls on reed mats lined up against one wall. Kan and Kepi walked along from sleeping mat to sleeping mat with nothing more to help them than the gray light of predawn. Kan stopped, and Kepi heard him suck in his breath.

The girl who lay before them had thick, wavy black hair that half covered her face. Kan squatted beside her head. Then he put a hand over her mouth.

The girl's eyes flew open, and she tried to pull his hand away.

Kan leaned over her. "Amisi, hello," he whispered. "It's Kan. Can you see me?"

She nodded.

Kan took his hand away.

"It's really you." Amisi put her hands on his cheeks, and her voice was full of joy. "Kan."

"I told you we'd see each other again. This is my friend Kepi. We need a place to stay for a while."

"Kepi?" Amisi's head jerked toward Kepi. "Your friend?"

"And Masud's friend, too."

"Masud? The metallurgist's son?"

"Adopted son. I'll tell you all about it. But you have to hide us first. Can you do that without telling anyone?"

"Look behind you."

Kepi and Kan turned around. Most of the other girls in the room had silently gathered behind them. The ones still on their sleeping mats watched with big eyes.

"We all work together here. Like sisters. You've found your hiding place. You're safe." Amisi smiled.

And with that smile, Kepi understood how very beautiful she was. But it was Kan who liked her best, not Masud. Kepi smiled, too.

28
THE WEAVERS' HOME

K epi stood over the large bucket. Yesterday, when no one was looking, she'd kicked that bucket out of impatience. She hated wasting time at the weavers' home. This was only her second day here, and already she thought she'd lose her mind if there was a third. She wanted to kick the bucket again now.

But she happened to look down and notice that her dress hem was turned up. She smoothed it and felt the five tiny tin bells hidden silent and safe within. Those special bells were the result of working at the metallurgist's. A feeling of calm started in her fingertips and ran through her body. Something good would come of her work at the weavers' home, too—something important. It would happen today, if she just kept her eyes open and recognized opportunity.

She leaned over the bucket with new attention. The pen shells in it came to a point at one end and fanned out at the other. They looked utterly ordinary. No one could guess from the outside what a treasure hid within. Fishermen collected them in the sea, which wasn't far from the delta. And they were dumped here in the bucket, in fresh river water, to die.

Kepi put her hands in and felt around. The ones that were dead already often opened on their own. If not, she opened them with her thumbnail. And if that didn't work, they were still alive, so she left them in the water longer. She collected more than fifty shells and brought them in a bowl to Amisi.

Amisi knelt on one side of the bowl, and Kepi knelt on the other. They pulled out the tuft of fibers embedded in the mollusks and teased apart the filaments, which were long and fine, much finer than Kepi's hair. They dropped the filaments into a second bowl filled with clean water and swished them about, then dropped them into a third bowl of water. Three washings were the rule.

But Amisi frowned. "This group of shells must have had a particularly sandy one in the lot. Feel."

Kepi ran some strands through her fingers. They seemed the same as always.

"See? The fibers still aren't quite clean." Amisi touched the bottom of her chin lightly with just the tip of her index finger. "I judge we need two more washings."

Amisi was too full of judgments, in Kepi's opinion. But she got clean water from the barrel, and they gave the filaments two more washings.

Then they held them up to the light, one by one, inspecting for color. Most strands were deep yellow, the color of the bronze cat the master metallurgist had made. Those were set aside in an additional bowl. Others were paler.

"This one," said Amisi, swinging a filament in front of Kepi's eyes, then draping it over the edge of the bowl. "And this one. I judge them both to be too pale. And these. I judge them all to be too pale." But fortunately, after that Amisi just gave quick nods at pale ones, so Kepi didn't have to sit on her hands to keep from pinching her.

Amisi filled yet another bowl with water and went to the jar on the dye shelf. She dropped saffron into the bowl. The water instantly became deep yellow. They put the palest filaments—the ones Amisi had passed her judgment on—into the dye.

Kepi sat down for a quick rest while Amisi went back to the bucket of pen shells and searched for more dead ones. That was how they worked, all morning long, all day long, alternating on some parts of the job and sharing on others. That was how six other pairs of girls worked right alongside them.

Kepi willed herself to sit still. She tried not to think of Masud walking the town, learning about the pharaoh, while she was stuck here.

At least Kepi liked these girls. They knew how to keep a secret. Amisi introduced Kepi to the mistress as an orphan, in need of a home and food in return for work. So a reed mat had been added to the floor for Kepi to sleep on. But there was no mat for Kan, because the mistress couldn't know about him or she'd kick him out. Boys weren't allowed. Last night Amisi gave up her sleeping mat to Kan, and she crawled in with Kepi. It worked well enough. When it came to meals, it seemed every girl saved a little bit for Kan. And the girls had stayed absolutely silent last night when Masud snuck in to report on his progress so far. It turned out the pharaoh wouldn't be giving a public audience for a month. Today Masud was going to try to find out where that would be. Kepi had nodded and hung her head, but inside she wanted to scream. She'd never last a month.

But Kepi should be grateful. These were generous girls, kind girls, secretive girls. Girls you could count on. The only thing that bothered her was that each of them had a tiny pouch tied flat against the inside of one wrist. When Kepi asked what it was, Amisi said she'd have to earn the knowledge. Secrecy could be annoying, too.

When Amisi judged that she and Kepi had cleaned enough filaments, they shifted to the next set of jobs. They rolled out long lengths of linen on tables set up end to end in the outdoor work area. They laid the cleaned filaments in straight lines on that cloth to dry. The filaments they had steeped in the saffron dye were just as shiny gold as the ones that were of natural color. None of the mistress's customers would ever know the difference.

As they worked, they talked. It wasn't like at the metallurgist's, where the master forbade the boys to talk. Maybe the mistress knew she couldn't stop girls from talking, so why try? Amisi wanted to hear the story of how Kepi came here. So Kepi made it brief. Then she asked, "How did you wind up at the weavers' home?"

Amisi blinked. "My parents were embalmers. Did you know that?"

"Yes."

Amisi gave a quick nod. "Scorpions were common in the embalming room. My father would throw the brains of some rich man in a corner, and a scorpion would run to eat them. If one ever ran toward my father, my mother would crush it. Usually there was only one scorpion. They seem to be solitary." Amisi's words matched the pace of her working hands. "One night when a scorpion ran at my father, my mother crushed it, but after she'd turned her back, another came and stung my father, and a third came and stung my mother. It isn't true that women can't be killed by scorpions. Everyone says it, but it isn't true.

Especially when she already has the breathing sickness."
She stopped talking.

All these orphans. All these slaves. "I'm sorry, Amisi."

Amisi patted the last filament flat and looked up.
"We can take a break now, while they dry." She went
back toward the sleeping room.

So Kepi went inside the shop where the weavers
worked. The weavers took the yarn that Kepi and Amisi
and the other girls made and wove it into the finest gold
cloth. They were just girls, too, and all the girls slept in
the same room. But there was a sense that they were of
higher status. Weaving was the premium job.

Kepi watched the weavers closely, looking for anything that might be an opportunity. Something was
going to happen today. It had to. A weaver put out her
hand for a yarn spindle that was just out of reach, and
Kepi leaped to her rescue. As she gave the spindle to
the weaver with one hand, she brushed her other hand
against the cloth on the loom. There was that magnifi-
cent texture again! It felt almost wooly, but much finer.
It was like the shadow of wool, the breath of it, the idea
of it. It was translucent and nearly transparent and softer
than the softest thing in the world. It seemed like it was
from beyond the human world. Something worthy of a
goddess.

The beauty of the cloth reminded Kepi of those

mornings with Menes when she'd awakened beside the water to a world all misty green. She'd thought of that mist as the gown of a goddess. But pen-shell cloth was even better. It seemed to move on its own, like a goddess dancing. This must be what the goddess Hathor's gown was made of. Kepi longed for a chance to hold the filmy substance to her cheek.

Amisi came up beside her and brushed her arm. Kepi looked at her as though woken from a trance. Amisi said, "We have to go back to work," and her tone was all business. Kepi was disappointed. The pity of such gloriously fine filaments was that it took only a moment in the open air for them to dry. Plus she'd thought that after Amisi had told her about her parents dying, they'd now act more like real friends. But Kepi obediently followed Amisi back to the tables.

They combed the filaments straight. Then each took a tapered stick—a spindle—and began spinning. The filaments got twisted together at the ends and spun into one long yarn thread.

This was the worst part of the job, for Kepi knew Amisi would pick on her. She twisted two filaments just like Amisi said, and tapped the little spindle just like Amisi said. And the spindle rotated, but not just like Amisi said.

Sure enough, Amisi soon stopped her own work,

poised her fingertip on her chin, and said, "I judge that to be too slow, Kepi. Go faster." So Kepi tried. Several minutes later, Amisi said the same thing. And Kepi tried harder. But several minutes after that, Amisi said the same thing. She'd probably say it twenty times before they finished.

Kepi spun that spindle as fast as she could. But Amisi stopped again and put her finger to her chin, and Kepi burst out, "You silly jackass. That's as fast as I can go."

"You're an idiot. First of all, jackasses are male. You can't call a girl that. Second, if you don't learn to spin right, you'll make inferior yarn and the mistress will beat you. And speed is necessary to pull the fibers hard enough and twist them tight enough to withstand anything."

"What a stupid thing to say—withstand anything."

"Pen-shell cloth is the strongest cloth in the world."

"Are you crazy? That cloth? It's soft. It's soft like . . . I don't know what it's like . . . it's deliciously soft. It must rip easily."

"Is that so?" Amisi took the end of the yarn she'd been spinning and handed it to Kepi. She walked back a distance, unwinding as she went. She stopped and said, "Go ahead, rip it."

Kepi grabbed the yarn and pulled. She glared at

Amisi and yanked harder.

"Don't stop with mere pulling. Try to rip it. Use anything you've got."

So Kepi tore at the yarn with her nails. She bit it. She grabbed a pottery shard and sawed at it. The shining golden line that stretched from her to Amisi stayed intact. "It's strong as crocodile skin."

"Stronger." Amisi lifted her chin as she walked back toward Kepi, winding up the yarn again. When she was face-to-face with Kepi, she said haughtily, "Turn that spindle faster." Then her eyes softened. "I was bad at first, too. You'll get better."

Kepi licked her lips. *Please, great goddess Nit, great god Set, great goddess Nekhbet, and especially especially great goddess Hathor, please, please, don't let me be here long enough to learn how to spin properly. Please let whatever is supposed to happen here happen fast.*

29
THE *WA'EB*

They spun as the sun made its way into the western sky. When they finished, the spindles were fat and full. They carried them inside to a shelf.

Amisi tapped Kepi's hand. "Come on," she whispered. She gave a quick nod and walked to the far corner and squatted there.

Kepi's frustration had reached the breaking point. The workday was going on just like yesterday—nothing new had happened. She had to get out of here—do something active, not just wait for Masud. The last thing she wanted to do was sit in the corner of the shop. But she looked out through the window just then and saw a shining arc in the sky. It was the crescent moon. You could see that arc in daylight whenever the god Tehuti took baboon form and held up the moon. Kepi was transfixed for a moment. The god Tehuti was telling her something. She turned back and went directly to Amisi and squatted beside her and looked around.

A tailor had come in. Amisi had explained that most tailors worked only with linen, because most people couldn't afford anything better. So the few tailors who worked with pen-shell cloth bought it for celebration dresses for the rich.

This tailor was accompanied by a man covered in white. He had a linen cloth wound around him, like any man. But instead of the cloth stretching just from his waist to his knees, it started under his armpits. Across the back of his shoulders was an extra swathe of material that came down on both sides and wound around his arms, all the way to his wrists. He wore white papyrus sandals instead of going barefoot. "Is that a holy man with the tailor?" Kepi whispered to Amisi.

"He's a *wa'eb*. He helps the *hem-netjer*, the priest, take care of the temple. And he runs errands. He comes here a few times a year to select cloth for the sacred robes worn in the temple. You're lucky to see him."

That man worked in a temple, and temples bought baboons! Kepi stared at him.

The tailor talked first to the mistress of the weavers. She nodded, but then she turned and boldly answered directly to the *wa'eb*. The tailor made no objection. He stepped back, allowing the *wa'eb* and the mistress to come closer together.

The *wa'eb* used his hands as he talked. He seemed to

be describing the size of something. Maybe something the size of a young baboon. Maybe the size Babu would be by now.

Kepi's pulse thumped in her ears. She had to know what they were talking about. She got to her feet and ran along the wall hunched over, trying to be inconspicuous. When she was immediately across from the *wa'eb*, she stopped and squatted again.

"He's little, yes, you're right. But he's growing bigger every day." The *wa'eb* put a hand on the small of his back as though it ached. "So I want it big enough for when he's an adult."

"Ah. Trying to be economical, I see." The mistress tilted her head to one side and looked off in the distance, as though lost in thought. "Hmmm. I fear that you're making a false economy. You'll wind up spending even more this way."

The *wa'eb* looked annoyed. "I know what I want."

"Yes, you do. But what you want isn't everything, is it?"

"What do you mean?"

"If the Sem priest has taken such a fancy to this baby, he'll want a small cloak that fastens at the neck and falls only to the bottom of the little creature's elbows. That way the animal can look trim and neat." The mistress shook her head, making her earrings fly. "No, I fear that if you buy only enough for a large cloak, the Sem priest will send you right back here to buy cloth for a small one."

The *wa'eb* frowned. "Well, if he does, I'll come back."

The mistress smiled with long yellow teeth. "By that time, the animal will undoubtedly have ruined the big cloak. Babies will be babies, even if they are sacred. Why, the creature will have dragged it on the ground and dirtied it beyond repair. And it must be spotless."

"It's not for ceremonies," said the *wa'eb* quickly. "We're having a white linen cloak made for temple ceremonies. Purity comes first, of course. This one will be for wearing before the pharaoh."

The pharaoh! Kepi leaned forward so far, she almost fell on her face.

"Well, I know that." The mistress blinked. and Kepi wondered if, in fact, she hadn't known. She couldn't have ever entered the temple herself—a working woman like her. She was plump like only mistresses and masters could be, but she was still just a commoner. "Of course. But the pharaoh may be even less forgiving of a dirty cloak in his home than the other gods and goddesses are in their home, no? So you'll wind up having to buy a third cloak for when the animal is full-size." She raised her eyebrows. "You'll do best in the long run if you buy enough for two cloaks now—one small and one big."

The *wa'eb*'s mouth twitched in a begrudging way, but he didn't object.

"In fact," said the mistress, with renewed enthusiasm, "it's a male, right?"

"Right," said the *wa'eb* warily.

"Well, then, he'll grow enormous. So you'll need a medium-size cloak, as well, for the middle stage, when he's no longer a baby, but not yet fully grown. You need enough for three cloaks."

The *wa'eb* swatted the air, as if to rid himself of a pesky insect. "I'll leave the amount to you and the tailor then. But I want to choose the bolt you cut from."

"Of course." The mistress went to the pile of bolts stacked up on the reed mats close to Kepi, so close that Kepi could smell the perfume on her hands—balsamum. Kepi moved even closer to her. The mistress gave a quick, sharp glance at Kepi, then went back to her task. She ran her finger along the bolts, as though searching. Her bracelets clinked together. "Here it is." She carried a bolt to the table near the west window. "Please, have a look. Take your time." She bowed and backed away, with hands folded at her bosom. That was when she looked Kepi full in the face and glared. She jerked her chin toward the outdoor work area.

But Kepi wasn't about to go back to work.

The mistress's eyes went along the wall to Amisi, still

squatting in the corner. Her mouth hardened into a thin line. Amisi came creeping over to Kepi and tugged on her arm. Kepi yanked herself free. She wasn't budging.

The tailor had unrolled a good length of cloth by now. He held it up to catch the afternoon sunlight.

The *wa'eb* blinked, clearly dazzled by the gold. It was brilliant. Shimmering. Perfect. "Yes," he said simply. And he went out the door, leaving the rest to the tailor.

Kepi ran after him, ignoring the mistress's angry splutterings behind her.

The *wa'eb* moved quickly for a man with a backache. He turned corners sharply. Kepi memorized the landmarks as they went. She needed to know how to get back to the weavers' home tonight. Kan would be waiting for her. And Masud would come to report on his findings of the day. She counted the blocks between turns.

Somehow the *wa'eb* had gotten far ahead of her. Kepi ran flat out. She didn't know the name of his temple or where it was. She mustn't lose him.

The *wa'eb* turned a corner, and by the time Kepi arrived there, he was out of sight. She looked down every side street. She peeked into every open window. He was gone.

30

THE TEMPLE

"The pharaoh's with that *wa'eb*. He said it. And I just bet Babu's with him, too. That's why he was buying the cloth, to make cloaks for my Babu." It was dark in the sleeping room, so Kepi couldn't make out anyone else's face clearly. She couldn't tell if they were convinced by what she'd said or not. "It has to be Babu," she said more firmly. "The god Tehuti made me eavesdrop on our mistress with the *wa'eb*. Why else would he have done that? If I can only find out where the *wa'eb* went, I can talk to the pharaoh and I can get Babu—both at once." Her voice shook with excitement. She'd given up hope of ever seeing her little baboon again, and now this: Babu would really be in her arms again, her sweet, dear Babu.

"You can't talk to the pharaoh, Kepi, I told you. You have to wait for the next public audience." It was Masud's voice. "But I know where the *wa'eb* went. There's only one temple that the pharaoh goes to. And I found out today that the Sem priests at that temple use baboons in the Opening of the Mouth and Eyes ritual."

"What's that?" asked Kan.

Kepi was grateful for the question. She didn't know about this ritual.

"Priests perform it on statues of dead people, so that they can smell and eat and see and taste and hear."

"All you need to do is make them breathe, too," said Kan, "and it sounds like you've brought them back from the dead."

From behind Kepi came the muffled laughter of a few girls. They were the slaves, and they were all foreigners—they didn't understand about Egyptian gods.

"I think they do breathe again. I just forgot to say that," mumbled Masud. "But they're dead. Really."

"So why do it?" asked Kan.

"This way their *ka* can enjoy the food offerings that their relatives bring to their tomb."

"Why do they need—"

"No more questions," said Masud. "Let me finish. The priest says prayers to four gods and does things with a special knife called a *psh-kef*, or something like that, and he uses bottles of perfume and burns smelly incense and I don't know what else. I only learned about all this today. Anyway, a baboon is part of it."

"What part?" asked Kepi, all senses alert for danger.

"The baboon holds an ostrich feather to the statue's

mouth. That's all I know." Masud was silent for a moment. "It's an important ritual," he added.

Good. Nothing about that seemed like it could hurt Babu.

"Too bad you can't do it to living people," said Kan. "My father fell from a cliff and went blind. I wish someone could give him back his sight."

Kepi looked sharply toward Kan's figure in the dark. His father must have had trouble doing his job after that injury. Just like Father. Maybe he figured Kan would be better off as a slave than starving. What a terrible choice. No one ever should have to trade away their child.

She remembered the boy and the legless man outside the gate of the metallurgy yard. They were starving. In all countries everywhere, people who get injured should be taken care of. Their families should be taken care of. What was wrong with the ruler of Kan's country? What was wrong with the pharaoh of Egypt?

"You can do the ceremony to living people," said Masud. "But only to the pharaoh. When a man gets crowned pharaoh, he becomes a god. And—"

"That's absurd," interrupted Kan. "Gods are the powers of nature. Dirt and sky, water and fire, sun and moon, and through it all the wind. A man is none of those things."

"This is Egypt, not your country," said Masud.

"So what? Do your gods have to be the same as stupid humans?"

"Watch what you say," said Kepi. "You don't know who might be listening."

Kan frowned, but he stopped talking, at least.

"Anyway," said Masud, "at the crowning of a pharaoh, they do the Opening of the Mouth and Eyes ritual so that his *ka* merges with his physical self forever."

"How did you find out all this?" asked Kepi.

Masud gave an apologetic little laugh. "The metalworkers told me."

"The slaves?" asked Amisi. "But they're foreign. They don't understand our gods."

"They listen. You know how it is. Whatever you can overhear helps make the day pass. One of them knew some things and another knew other things, and pretty soon everyone had something to say—and it all came together."

"Wait." Kepi reached out and took hold of Masud's arm. "Did you tell them about Kan and me?"

Masud shook his head. "I asked questions and they answered them, and no one even wondered why I was asking. They were too busy worrying about how the laborers on Pharaoh Khufu's new pyramid are striking over garlic."

"Garlic?"

"Their daily ration isn't high enough. They're getting sick. So they staged a strike. Pharaoh Khufu has threatened to gather up everyone's male slaves and make them finish his pyramid. And he's cruel, everyone knows that. The boys are afraid."

This city was full of trouble. Mean masters and a meaner pharaoh. In Kepi's home village slaves were treated nicely. A lump formed in her throat so big, it hurt her ears. "Let's go get Babu tonight." And I'll talk to the pharaoh at the same time, she thought. She couldn't possibly wait a whole month for the public audience. Already she feared she'd be getting home too late to save her family.

"We can't," said Masud. "The priests will be home asleep with their families—and Babu will be wherever the *wa'eb* sleeps. But we can go to the temple and hide and wait till morning."

"And what will we do in the morning?" asked Kan.

"As soon as I see Babu, I'll call to him," said Kepi. "He'll jump on my head and we can run away and meet up later."

"They'll chase you," said Amisi.

"I'm fast."

"Plus," said Kan, "if there's three of us, we can all run in different directions, and they'll break up following us—it won't be everyone following only Kepi. It's better that way."

"Then I'm coming, too," said Amisi. "One more person for them to chase."

"What if you're not back before the mistress calls everyone to the morning meal?" asked Kepi. "You'll get in trouble."

"I don't care. If Kan's helping, I'm helping."

The four of them sat immobile a moment. Kepi felt the air grow thick around them, as though it was binding them together like a giant swathe of cloth. The other three had known each other for a long time, but Kepi was new to the group. Yet the air was pulling all of them together equally. They had vowed to spend the future together. Masud would come to Kepi's village. And Masud had invited Kan. And Kepi was pretty sure that wherever Kan went, Amisi would want to go. But all of that was just plans—just talk about the future. It was very different to talk about this moment here. About doing something tonight. And something so dangerous. Somehow their bond was strong enough that the three of them were willing to take this risk for Kepi. She didn't understand how it had happened, but she was overcome with gratitude that made her feel all melty, like a candle at the end of its life. "Thank you." She wished she could show them how much she meant it.

Without another word, Kan and Masud and Amisi and Kepi snuck out the door on tiptoe. They slipped out into the street, following Masud. He led them a long way; the dark made it feel endless. Finally the houses stopped and they came to high walls enclosing a huge temple. Masud stopped and sucked in his top lip behind his bottom teeth.

"What's wrong?" whispered Kepi. "Anybody is allowed within the walls, no matter how poor. It's just the temple itself we can't enter."

"I know." Masud turned to them. "Listen. There's nowhere to hide in the temple yard. I looked earlier. But there's a secret chamber under the temple. It's not really like entering the temple itself."

"How do you know?" asked Amisi.

"I saw men come out of there."

"But how do you know it's not like entering the temple itself?"

"I don't know for sure. But I watched. It seems only the people who take care of the temple go down there. The main Sem priest doesn't."

No one spoke.

"All right," said Kepi at last. "Let's go."

She ran through the wall entrance, across the yard,

and to the side door. The other three ran with her, like the truest of friends. Masud opened the door, and they looked down the stairs into blackness.

Kepi turned her face to the sky. *Great goddess Hathor, smile on us, please. We're leaving your moonlight. But please don't let us out of your sight. We need you, dear goddess. We draw strength from you.*

They filed down the stairs. It was a long way down.

The chamber was larger than Kepi expected. And the stone walls were cold. The four of them huddled together.

"Whose temple is this?" Kepi asked Masud.

"The goddess Sekhmet."

A shiver shot through Kepi. Sekhmet was mean. Vicious even. Kepi rubbed her hands together to take off the chill that enveloped her. "And who are the four gods?"

"What?"

"You said four gods are prayed to in the Opening of the Mouth and Eyes ritual. Which ones?

"Tehuti, Set, Horus, and Dunawy."

This was better news. Tehuti loved baboons, and maybe it really was he who had come as that giant ibis to encourage Kepi when she was chasing the Nubian boys, and for sure it was he who had let her see the crescent moon so she would eavesdrop on the *wa'eb*. And

Set, well, he was Kepi's personal patron. He'd come as a crocodile to warn the crew—with disastrous effects, but that was his nature; Set was vengeful. Horus was the most important of all the gods, and he was the patron of young men. So he should want to take care of Masud and Kan, at least. And he was Hathor's husband, so he'd care about Kepi, too. Those three gods sounded very good indeed.

The only mystery was Dunawy. Dunawy was the god with extended wings. He protected flying things. Kepi didn't see how he would care at all about Babu or any of them. But she didn't see any reason he would be against them, either.

Inside her heart Kepi prayed. *Please, Tehuti, Set, Horus, and Dunawy. I need to talk with the pharaoh. I know he comes often to this temple, so please let me find him here. He did something very wrong to Father, and he's done lots of wrong things to lots of people. I need to tell him, so he'll change his ways, and so I can save my family and maybe lots of other families. You care about people—if I do this, I'm serving you. It's true. I've never looked at it like that before, but now I can see it's true.*

And, please, oh, please please help me get Babu back. I know he's working here now, in this temple. But he's just a baby. He needs me. Please agree that he belongs with me. I'll teach him to pray. Every day. To all four of you. And to Sekhmet, too. So he'll serve the gods no matter what. Please allow me to find him. Please allow me to take him home.

31
AT LAST

The hours passed. There were no windows. Light couldn't penetrate this room unless the door was open. How would they know when dawn came?

Kepi felt her way carefully, past the sleeping bodies of her three friends and up the stairs to the temple yard. She would open the door just a little. Enough to let in a sliver of light when morning finally came but, hopefully, not enough to alert people outside that they were there.

But when she cracked the door open, the rosy haze of morning greeted her. Already! A man walked past, covered in white cloth with white papyrus sandals. Kepi quickly closed the door, raced down the steps, and tripped and tumbled all the way to the bottom.

"Who's that?"

"What happened?"

"I fell." Kepi pulled herself to her feet. Her arm hurt. "It's dawn. And a priest is already here. Outside our door. We can't get out without him seeing us—and if he sees us, how can we sneak up on them?"

"Come over here, Masud," called Kan. "Hurry. At this end of the room there's another staircase."

Kepi heard Masud stumble as he crossed the room. "All right. I'll go up and see what's at the top."

Everyone hushed.

"There's a door," came Masud's voice again, finally. "It opens into the temple. And the temple's still empty."

"Let's go hide up there," came Kan's voice. "Then we can see what's going on."

"We can't enter the temple," said Kepi. "Ordinary people aren't pure enough."

"I'm not Egyptian," said Kan. "No god can expect a foreigner to follow the rules. And you three have come to rescue Babu. That's an honorable goal. If the gods don't understand that, they're crazy."

"Kan didn't mean that last thing," Kepi said loudly. "Please, gods and goddesses, whoever is listening. Kan can be a silly jackass. Ignore that last thing he said, please. But the rest of what he said sounds right. Doesn't it? Please show us what to do."

"You believe nothing happens just by chance, right?" asked Kan.

"Right," said Kepi.

"Then the gods already showed us what to do," said Kan. "They showed us this staircase."

Kepi sensed they all agreed. All of them must have, for the four of them climbed the staircase together. They came out into the cavernous temple, where the air was a soft pale gray. They flattened themselves against the side wall and sank to squatting. Kepi looked up at the ceiling. It was blue with yellow stars. Glorious.

Only a moment later, the front door of the temple opened. A shaft of light cut through the center of the room. A procession of men came in. All dressed in white. All wearing white papyrus sandals. The one in the lead had a leopard skin draped at a slant across his chest and back, held in place by a cord at one shoulder. The leopard head and tail flopped as he walked. That was the Sem priest. Behind him came two men with white robes on top of their clothing. The *hem-netjer*, the priests. At the rear was the *wa'eb* Kepi had seen at the weavers'. They intoned the morning hymn, praying to the goddess Sekhmet to awaken in peace.

The pharaoh wasn't there.

And neither was Babu.

Kepi and Masud and Kan and Amisi were taking this terrible chance for nothing.

The holy men walked to a small sanctuary at the center of the room, and the Sem priest broke the seal on the sanctuary door. The statue of the goddess Sekhmet was revealed. The Sem priest said a prayer over the statue,

four times. Then the *wa'eb* reached inside the sanctuary and took out a piece of cloth and a jar. He poured
from the jar onto the cloth and handed it to the Sem
priest. Then he took out more cloth and poured again,
so the *hem-netjer* also had them. He stood back as the
three higher priests rubbed the statue of Sekhmet. The
jar must have held oil, for the statue shone now. They
took out a blue linen dress from the sanctuary and
slipped it over the statue's head. They added a red linen
cloak. As the Sem priest adorned the statue with jewelry,
one *hem-netjer* applied kohl around her eyes, and the
other dabbed her everywhere with the scent of myrrh,
so strong Kepi could inhale it from her hiding spot way
over in the shadows.

The *wa'eb*, meanwhile, had left the temple. But he
came back now, lugging an enormous basket of food.
He brushed off a reed mat and spread a linen cloth on
it. Then he set out a roasted duck and a leg of lamb and
boiled greens. He put a jar on each corner of the mat.
And he made a pile of dried fruits—figs and dates and
raisins—in the very center.

All four priests stepped back and waited. Kepi knew
about this part. The goddess was eating her fill. Then
the priests would take the remains away to be distrib-
uted at the shrines of other gods and goddesses around
the city. And whatever remained at the end would go to

the priests and their families. The smell of the food was heavenly. Kepi's mouth watered. She'd had nothing to eat since the morning before.

But now another man appeared at the temple door. From his dress, Kepi knew he was a *wa'eb*. And he carried a bamboo cage.

It was Babu! The baboon had grown, but she recognized him instantly.

Kepi almost cried out. But a hand on her arm gripped her tight. She pressed her lips together and watched.

The *wa'eb* brought the cage to the Sem priest. He got down on one knee and opened it. Babu came flying out and landed on the priest's head, where he chattered happily and picked a few fleas from the man's hair. Then he leaped from there down to the reed mat. He grabbed a date and chomped on it. All the priests left, closing the door to the temple behind them.

Everyone was silent for a moment. Then Kepi jumped up. "Babu," she cried. "Oh, Babu!"

The little baboon leaped onto the head of the statue of Sekhmet and screamed in alarm.

"Babu, it's me. Don't you know me? Don't you remember?"

Babu stared at her.

The others came forward now.

"Can we eat?" asked Kan.

"No," said Kepi. "You mustn't. This is food for the goddess."

"She's a statue."

"But the statue is alive. That's what the Sem priest's prayers did. They called back the goddess to her statue."

"I don't see her eating anything."

"Maybe she hasn't arrived yet," said Kepi.

"The baboon's eating a date," said Kan. "I'm eating one, too. Oh, it's wonderful."

"Stop!" Kepi looked back at Babu. "I came to take you home, my dear Babu." She reached out.

Babu grimaced, showing his teeth. And they had grown big. Big as a dog's. He didn't have fangs yet, but it was clear his jaw was strong. His head was larger now, too, and it had developed a droop.

"He looks like he'll bite," said Masud.

"Babu." Kepi shook her head slowly. "Babu, my baby." She stretched her hands out toward him again. "Come to me."

Babu barked.

"He doesn't remember you, Kepi," said Masud. "I guess a couple of months is a long time in a little baboon's life."

"But be glad," said Kan. "He's happy here."

"How happy could he be, locked in a cage?"

"That's probably only where he sleeps," said Amisi. "You saw how he jumped to the Sem priest's head. He likes him. And you see the food they give him. He's got a good life, Kepi." She looked at the food. "Is it really good, Kan?"

Kan handed her a piece of meat. "We're hungry. And who knows when we'll have food again? If the gods care at all about us, they'll want us to eat."

Masud took a piece, too. The three of them ate.

But Kepi couldn't. Tears rolled down her cheeks. "I love you, Babu." And then she remembered. She curled up the edge of her dress and felt inside the hem and pulled out the ostrich feather. "Here, dear Babu. They say that you'll help in the Opening of the Mouth and Eyes ritual. And you'll use an ostrich feather. Use this one. Please." She held it out toward Babu.

The little monkey watched her.

Kepi sang. She sang a fieldworkers' song. "Do you remember that one, Babu?" She sang another. "Do you remember that one? You used to dance with me to them." She poured all her love into the songs. And all the while she held the ostrich feather out to him.

When she stopped singing, Babu leaped to Kepi's head, snatched the feather from her hand, and leaped back onto the statue's head.

"They're coming back!" said Masud. "I hear them outside."

They ran to the walls and hid in the shadows again.

The procession of priests entered, but it was different now; a new man led them. His white robe was so transparent, Kepi could see the muscles of his arms and chest and legs. Around his waist wrapped a skirt with many tiny pleats and a bull tail hanging down so low in the back that it swung between his calves. In his right hand was a palm frond that he pressed to his chest. But what made her gasp was his headdress. It was tall and of white linen, and mounted at the front of it, above the strip of leather around his forehead, was the *uraeus*—the royal cobra. Everybody knew that only one person wore such a headdress. This was the *nemes* of the pharaoh.

Masud's fingers closed around Kepi's arm so tight, she almost yelped. "We're in the sacred temple. If you reveal us, we'll be punished. Severely. You know of his cruelty."

That was true. But this was Kepi's chance, at last. "Stay hidden," said Kepi. "I mean it. If any of you come out, I'll hate you forever." And she burst from the shadows, running straight for the pharaoh.

The priests turned from gaping at the half-eaten food offering to gaping at this little girl. Kepi streaked through the beam of sunlight.

"Pharaoh Khufu, your majesty," said Kepi. She could hardly catch her breath. "I must speak with you."

"A child in the temple!" Pharaoh Khufu's voiced boomed. His face wrinkled in anger. White hairs here and there on his head looked like the hottest flames. He turned to the Sem priest. "How did you let her get in here?"

"The gods let me," said Kepi. It had to be true. How else could it be that they'd found Babu in this huge city? How else could it be that Kepi was actually in front of the pharaoh, when she was nothing more than a village girl? "I have to talk to you about justice. You've done bad things."

"She's eaten the goddess's food. This is a grave crime. Take her away. I'll decide later whether she's to be drowned or beheaded."

The *wa'eb* grabbed Kepi from behind.

"No! I didn't eat anything! Not a single bite!"

Babu barked and jumped onto Kepi's head. He waved the ostrich feather in the *wa'eb*'s face and bared his teeth. The *wa'eb* let out a little shriek and stepped back.

"You see?" said Kepi. "The sacred baboon wants me to speak. That means the goddess Sekhmet wants me to speak."

Pharaoh Khufu jerked his head toward the Sem priest.

The Sem priest shrugged. "This baboon has already proven himself an obedient servant, your majesty. He's smarter than the others. And that feather . . . I don't know where he got it. But it's a sacred ostrich feather, I'm sure. Maybe the goddess Sekhmet gave it to him."

"Smell her breath," ordered Pharaoh Khufu.

The Sem priest put his face to Kepi's mouth. She opened it wide and breathed hot on him. "I can't smell meat or greens or fruits. I don't believe she's eaten in a while."

"Speak!" ordered Pharaoh Khufu.

"You treat your pyramid workers badly."

Pharaoh Khufu's kohl-ringed eyes were large and penetrating. "That's false! I clothe them. I feed them. I've paid them radishes and onions and leeks and bread worth hundreds of talents of silver already."

"But when a worker gets injured . . ."

"My surgeons take care of any injured worker!" boomed Pharaoh Khufu.

"Then you send him home with nothing. He can't go back to his old work. He's ruined. His family is ruined. And sometimes workers die, and their families get nothing. Orphans wind up living like slaves. And slaves—you don't treat slaves right in this city. All this is unfair."

"You understand nothing about justice and injustice.

I'm the one who judges what is just or unjust."

"Not in the afterlife. Everyone is judged in the after-life. Even the pharaoh. You will be judged poorly." Kepi didn't know what happened to you if you were judged poorly in the afterlife. Neither Father nor Mother had ever told her. The judgment alone had been threat enough for her and Nanu to behave well. But she went on boldly. "You must give every injured worker money. Enough for the rest of his life. You must do the same for the families of workers who die. Whether they are free or slaves. And you have to take care of orphans."

"Nonsense! Stop talking!" Pharaoh Khufu looked at the goddess's altar. He beat the palm frond against his chest. "We must offer our thanks. Like always."

They all said a prayer of thanks.

Pharaoh Khufu looked at the *wa'eb*. "What are you waiting for? Clean up."

The *wa'eb* quickly gathered the remains of the meal into the enormous basket. Then the priests sprinkled water over the statue and the sanctuary. They set some-thing on the floor and lit incense. The Sem priest closed and resealed the sanctuary door. He looked at Pharaoh Khufu. "What do you want us to do with the child?"

"I haven't decided. Put her in the downstairs cham-ber for now."

The Sem priest tapped the top of his head. Babu

quickly jumped to him.

Pharaoh Khufu and the three higher priests left, taking Babu with them.

The *wa'eb* pulled Kepi roughly by the arm to the very door she'd come out of that morning. He opened it and flung her down the stairs. He shut the door. A moment later she heard the temple doors close. And a moment after that, the chamber door reopened, and Masud, Kan, and Amisi rushed down the stairs to Kepi.

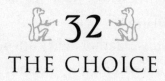

32
THE CHOICE

"We have to get out of here," said Kepi.

"We can't," said Kan. "There are still priests in the temple yard. I peeked out the door at the top of the entrance steps."

Kepi bit the side of her fist in desperation. "Go back upstairs and hide in the shadows of the temple. You three can wait till they've taken me away, and then you can sneak out safely."

"We won't leave you, Kepi," said Masud. "We heard what you said to the pharaoh. You spoke for all of us. We're united."

"Don't be crazy. I'm in trouble. But you're not. No one knows you three are here."

"Did you actually say no one knows the three of them are here?" came a voice reverberating through the black air inside the underground chamber. "We're divinity. Are you adding insult to injury?"

Kepi and Masud and Kan and Amisi immediately

huddled together, trembling.

"Don't be harsh with them," came another voice. "They made a mistake."

"Stay out of this, Hathor. They ate my food."

"They're children and they were hungry. Besides, you never eat it."

"That's no excuse. They shouldn't even have been in my temple."

"They were here for an important reason, Sekhmet. They're good children, pure at heart," said the goddess Hathor. "The boys are metalworkers, so your husband, Seker, cares about them. And one of the girls is special to me. She prays to me all the time. You could simply—"

"It's my temple! I decide what happens to them."

"Goddesses," Kepi dared to say, "please . . ."

"Hush!" shouted Sekhmet. "You're the child who talks too much! You went on and on with the pharaoh. But his meting out of punishment will be nothing compared to mine."

"Now wait just a minute," said Hathor. "We have to see what the other four gods have to say. The girl invoked them, after all."

"Never! Anytime Horus gets involved in things, he bosses everyone, plus you have sway over him. And Set can't be trusted to be impartial, not with this girl. And who cares what Tehuti and Dunawy think, anyway?"

"The child invoked them! You can't ignore that."

"And we're already here," came a chorus of deep voices.

"No!" shrieked Sekhmet.

"Look," came the reasonable voice of Hathor, "why don't those of you who want to argue go upstairs to the temple? I'll stay with the children down here."

"They can't just go back to the life they had," spluttered Sekhmet. "At least the three of them who ate my food. No matter what, that cannot be."

"I'm sure everyone agrees about that," said Hathor. "Go upstairs. Go on. Go confer and figure out what to do."

There was a moment of silence.

"Is there any other god left here?" came Hathor's voice, seeming much smaller now in the heavy dark.

"I am."

"Ah, Dunawy. I'm glad it's you. You're the god of boatmen, and this girl child was on boats for months."

"Hathor," said Kepi quietly, "this is my fault. Please let the others go."

"Of course it's your fault. We had a different plan for you, Nit and Set and I, but then you got those other children involved."

So it was true. The goddess Hathor had been with her all along. "I didn't mean to mess up your plan. I didn't even understand you had a plan, really."

"It's not your job to understand the gods."

"I'm so sorry." Kepi's voice broke. "The others didn't do anything wrong. Please let them go."

"Stop fretting, Kepi. I have to think. And fast, before the other gods make a decision. I can't go against them once they announce a decree."

Amisi whimpered. Kan groaned. Masud swallowed loudly.

"I'm sorry," Kepi said. "I'm so, so sorry."

"I think the dark is getting everyone way too sad," said Hathor. "Let me fix that." Instantly the room glowed with moonlight, though it was full morning outside.

The first thing Kepi saw seemed to be a shadow of a bird. It had to be Dunawy. His nose was beaklike. His wings were folded. His arms ended in bird talons. He fastened one eye directly on the four children.

Kepi turned her head away, and there was Hathor behind them. She too was like a shadow, but a glorious one. She was more beautiful than the most beautiful woman Kepi could ever imagine. She looked as though she was made of milk, all soft and white and rich. Her myrrh perfume filled Kepi's lungs and made her feel as though she'd float away.

Amisi suddenly stood. She untied the small pouch from her wrist and took another one from inside her shift. "Here, everyone. This may be our last chance. So do what I do. Stand up, Kepi." Kepi stood up. Amisi handed her the other pouch. "I was sure you'd earn it, so I prepared one for you. It's just luck I brought it along."

Kepi watched as Amisi pulled out two little squares from her pouch. She handed one square to Kan. Then she unfolded the other one. She unfolded and unfolded and unfolded. The little square turned out to be a swathe of cloth. She wrapped it once around her head. Then she twirled and sparkled gold in the silvery moonlight. It was pen-shell cloth! The cloth was so fine, it could be wrapped up to almost no size at all! Why, it could fit in a dried scarab shell.

Kepi opened her pouch and handed a square to Masud. Then the three of them unfolded their squares and tied the cloth around their heads. And they twirled, too. It was like diving into the cleanest water. Kepi could feel it, but it gave way to her, almost as though she was moving through it. It was heavenly. She felt she had become her own *akhu*—her own radiant, shining dot to whirl among the gods.

The four of them were dancing lights. It was as though sparks of energy flew around the room, igniting new ones.

"Thank you, Amisi," breathed Kepi. "This is marvelous."

"Marvelous," said Kan. "That's what you said when

you first heard my tin bells clink together." He opened his pouch and threw tiny bells into the air.

The children caught them and set them clinking. The whole room resounded with tinkling bells.

If only this could last forever, this feeling of lightness and beauty.

"That's it," sang out Hathor. "Exactly! All right, children. Your intentions were good. I know because I listened to your thoughts all along. I can handle Sekhmet's wrath. So you have a choice. First, I could let you out through the side door into the yard and make sure no one sees you. You could go on with your lives. Not back to your old lives, Amisi and Kan and Masud, because Sekhmet has already forbidden that. And your old lives are a shambles now, anyway. But back to Kepi's village, however you manage to do it, to whatever new life you can form there."

"That sounds great," said Kan. "I'll work for Masud, like we planned."

"But what's the other choice?" asked Kepi.

"You can be mine."

Kepi walked toward the goddess. Prickles ran up her neck and cheeks. She remembered mornings on the river, wishing she could belong to Hathor. "What does that mean?"

"I am the goddess of the night sky. I am the goddess

of music. You will be my little shining musical helpers on earth, forever and ever. When people pray to me from their sleeping mats, you can ring those little things— those bells—till they fall asleep. They'll love me even more! And the four of you have a strong sense of right and wrong, so you can help in other ways, too. I'll give you a special gift: You'll be able to see the future. That way, if you don't like what's about to happen, you can warn people, so they change what they're doing."

"If I had been able to see the future, everything would have been different," said Amisi. Her voice sounded strange, stronger. "I take the second choice. If Kan will, too."

"I will," said Kan.

"Kepi?" said Masud.

If Kepi had been able to see the chunk of limestone about to fall, she could have saved her father's foot. If she had seen the sandstorm about to come, she could have made Menes stay in town until after it had passed. There were so many wonderful things she could do with that gift. But still. "None of you have families worrying about you, waiting for you to come home," said Kepi. "I do, though."

"True," said Amisi. "Family is the best treasure."

"My father, my mother, my sister." A huge lump formed in Kepi's throat. "I love them so much. I love how we are when we're together."

"There are different kinds of families." Masud spoke softly and gently. "Some you're born into. Some you choose. We can be your new family, Kepi. We're in this together."

We're in this together. Words that rolled in Kepi's heart like a prayer. That's what she had felt last night, when her three new friends had decided to risk everything for her. What truer family could there ever be? It was like Father said—for every joy there is a price to be paid. But this joy just might break her heart. "Can we have time to think about it, great goddess Hathor?"

"Once the others make a decision about your fate, I can't help you any longer. And I can see their discussion is close to ended. You have to hurry. It's now or never."

Kepi had just lost Babu. And now she was being asked to lose Father and Mother and Nanu. She'd never known such agony. And the pharaoh would never change. All this had been for nothing.

Within her, a voice spoke. It wasn't her father, and it wasn't a god. It was just Kepi, talking to Kepi. What you do doesn't matter so much as what you learn from doing it.

What had Kepi learned? Maybe nothing good. Maybe all she'd learned was that you can't make other people change. You can't make them be good and act decent. You can only control yourself. You can only be decent yourself.

Life was full of danger. And Egypt was riddled with injustice. The pharaoh was wrong: Kepi understood a lot about justice and injustice. These past months had taught her well. If Kepi could see the future, she could stop some of the bad things from happening. Not all bad things— she couldn't be everywhere all the time. But maybe a lot of things. She knew that now. That was her choice—to take the responsibility or not. And if she did, she wouldn't be alone. She'd have her new family. Forever. She'd be like air and water and earth—continuing beyond the cycle of life. It would be like becoming part of nature. Really, for a girl like Kepi, what could be better?

Kepi closed her eyes and dared to be as true a friend as Masud and Amisi and Kan were: "I take the second choice, too."

"Wise children," said Hathor. "But there's one more thing. You must be tiny. I am the great light—not you. I am the goddess; you are just helpers. You must be small enough to stand on the tip of a man's finger."

"Wait!" called Masud. "If we're that small, we'll get crushed by anything that walks past."

"Not with wings, you won't," said Dunawy. "Feel

behind your shoulders. You're like insects now—you have both legs and wings. Just not the usual number."

And they were. They were like click beetles. Ha! Kepi saw the circle closing.

The four of them were little fluttery things. Little fluttery naked things, for their clothes had not shrunk with them and so had fallen in heaps. Kepi picked up the pen-shell cloth that had been tied around her head. It was so light that, even minuscule as she was, she could lift it. She tied it into a sheath around herself.

Amisi did the same. And Masud and Kan made *shenti*s of their pen-shell cloth.

"The door's open," said Hathor. "You are my little beloved ones, my *meri*. And you are so beautiful—*nefer*. I want people to think of both things when you light up for them—love and beauty. So I'll call you my *feri*. Make people laugh in happiness. Honor me. Go now."

33
LIGHTS AND BELLS

The four of them perched high in a sycamore right outside the temple yard walls. They had flown here in silence, and now they sat in silence.

"Does anyone feel dizzy looking down?" asked Kan. "I used to hate heights. I remember climbing in the mountains when I was little and crying in terror. But now I feel wonderful."

"I can make just one wing move. Look." Masud fluttered one wing. He almost rocked right off the branch. He caught himself and laughed.

"You know," said Amisi, "I was one of the best workers, but the mistress would never have let me move up from a spinner to a weaver because I'm an outcast. She'd have always treated me nasty. Now I'm one of Hathor's helpers. What did she call us? *Feri*. I'm a *feri*. And I'm lovely. And no one will treat me nasty again."

"Who knows where I would have been sold next," said Kan. "The master scorned me and so did everyone else. But now . . ." He blushed and hesitated. "Now I'm with Amisi."

Amisi sidled along the branch, pushing aside the shiny green leaves, and settled closer to Kan.

"The master didn't scorn me," said Masud. "But he never loved me. I know what real love is. My father said the sun rose and set in me. He told me stories about the gods all the time. He wanted me to be good and happy. That's what it means to be a parent—you're supposed to love a child, whether or not the child is adopted. The master didn't know anything about being a father. I would have spent my life never ever being with anyone who cared about me."

"I care about you," said Kepi.

"We all do," said Amisi.

"See?" Masud smiled. "Look how lucky we are."

Kepi's eyes stung with gratitude. These were good friends, a new family. Like Amisi said, family was the best treasure. But now she closed her eyes. The hole in her heart was vast. "I have to go see my mother and father and sister. I have to say good-bye."

"I'll go with you," said Masud.

"We can all go together," said Kan. "And, then, do you think . . . ?"

"Yes," said Kepi. "Yes, yes. We can go to your country and you can see your old family, too."

"But how will you say good-bye?" asked Amisi. "We're so tiny, will they even know it's a voice? All people hear when an insect talks is a whir or a buzz."

"We have the bells," said Kan.

"But they're heavy," said Amisi.

Kepi looked down in dismay at the base of the tree. They had each carried only one bell with them when they'd left the temple chamber, and they'd set them under the tree.

"We can hammer them flat and make lots of new, smaller bells from them," said Kan.

"With what?" asked Masud. "We're too small to lift a hammer."

"I bet if we all work together, we can swing a hammer. And once the metal is thin enough, we can use pebbles to shape the bells. We can just fly over to the metallurgist's and do it when the shop's empty."

Amisi smiled her beautiful smile. "Just fly over there. The sound of that is so funny. Just fly on over. But it's right. That's what we do now; we fly."

So that's what they did. From those four bells they made four hundred teeny-tiny bells, and they stashed almost all of them in niches under an eave of the metallurgist's shop. Then they each took ten and tied them into a fold of the pen-shell cloth that covered them.

It took them no time at all to reach Kepi's village, for

feris aren't bound by human time.

The others waited on the roof while Kepi flew around the outside of her home. She could hardly believe what she saw. When Father had started baking bread, they used to make one row of fires for the baking embers— and a short one, at that. But now she saw six long rows. Father must be selling bread to the entire village. Maybe word had spread to nearby villages—maybe even to the big city of Wetjeset-Hor. People must come from everywhere for Father's bread. Ha! Herb bread must be delicious, after all. Beside the old baking disks were new ones, shaped like fish and triangles and birds. Kepi imagined the village children's delight at munching those whimsical breads.

But she couldn't fly around outside forever. She had to go inside. She had to face these people who she loved. Kepi flew through a window.

Father stood by the carpet, where a loaf of bread and a jug of beer lay. He wasn't eating. He wasn't doing anything, really, just leaning on his crutch. Grief had aged his face. His cheeks hung just a little. His eyes looked heavy.

"I love you," Kepi said.

Father didn't even move. Amisi must have been right—he couldn't hear her.

Kepi flew around Father's head.

Father blinked.

Kepi circled him again.

Father leaned back and swatted at the air.

Kepi flew just out of reach and jingled her bells.

"What's that?" Father's eyes followed as Kepi flitted around the room. "Are you a scarab?"

Kepi jingled her bells. Then she landed on the carpet and climbed onto the loaf of bread.

"Jingle. Jingle." Father's mouth opened in wonder. He leaned over. He shook his head slowly, side to side. "You're a point of light. But I think I see a face behind that glow. A face I know. Could it be? Is that you? Is that my Kepi? My little jingle-jangle?"

Kepi couldn't have spoken now, even if Father could hear her voice. She was crying too hard. She jingled her bells.

A tear rolled down Father's cheek. "We've missed you so much."

Kepi jingled her bells.

"I've never seen anything like you before. You're a star that's come to earth. A tiny, wonderful, singing star. The very sight of you makes me happy." And then he straightened up. "Oh. I have to tell your mother and your sister. Right away. They have to see you. Come.

Come, Kepi, my love, my jingle-jangle."

So Kepi sat on Father's shoulder as he slowly hopped his way with a cane toward the river, where Mother and Nanu were scrubbing laundry.

"Look," called Father. "Look look!"

Mother and Nanu jumped to their feet in alarm. They came running. "Is something wrong, Father?" asked Mother. She, too, looked so old, so thin, so fragile.

And Nanu's eyes behind her were liquid with a sadness far beyond her years.

"Our daughter's come back."

"What? Kepi? Where?" Mother grabbed Father's arms and clung there. "Where is she?"

"Here, on my shoulder."

Mother stared. Nanu came up behind her and stared. Kepi jingled her bells.

Mother's mouth fell open, but she didn't speak.

"That's Kepi?" said Nanu. She came closer and blinked. "Yes. Yes, I can see her funny face. I can see the face of my sister. Oh, Kepi. Kepi, you came back."

Kepi jingled her bells.

"She's a spark of light," said Mother slowly.

"What silly thing did you do to turn yourself into light?" asked Nanu.

Kepi jingled her bells.

"You won't believe what's happened while you've

been gone. Everyone trades for Father's bread rather than making their own. Some leave us fish or pots or cloth. Others work Father's fields in exchange for bread. Mother and I don't have to do fieldwork anymore. And . . ." Nanu twirled around. "I'm getting married in a month."

Kepi jingled and jingled her bells.

"I love that sound," said Mother. "It's so high and tinkly. I want it every day. Do you hear me, Kepi? I want to hear that sound every day for the rest of my life."

"Me, too," said Nanu.

Kepi untied the knot in the tip of her pen-shell shift. She flew round and round Mother, till Mother opened her hands in confusion. Then Kepi dropped two bells in her palm.

"What's this?" Mother raised her hand to her eyes. "Two minuscule metal bowls."

"I want them," said Nanu.

Mother held her hand over Nanu's and dropped in the bells, which clinked against each other as they fell. "Ah, that's the sound."

Kepi dropped two more bells into Mother's now-empty palm.

Father held out his palm. Kepi dropped bells into it.

"So this is your voice, Kepi." Mother's tears fell on the bells and made them shine. "Every morning and every night when I say I love you, I'll flick these little bowls together so I can hear you saying you love me, too."

Kepi flew right at Mother's face. She couldn't stop herself. But Mother seemed to understand. She closed her eyes. Kepi kissed her wet lashes.

Then she kissed Nanu and Father.

"Thank you for coming back, Kepi." Nanu kissed her fingertips and blew the kiss to Kepi. "You made us happy."

There was nothing left to do. Kepi flew in a circle above them, wanting so much to stay—but she was a *feri*. She didn't belong here anymore. She jingled and jingled and jingled her bells.

Nanu shook her head. Then she sighed. "You're leaving?"

"She has to," said Father. "I don't know what's next for Kepi, but I know it's important. And we have to be happy for her."

"Oh, Kepi," called Mother. "Visit us now and then, sweet daughter."

And she would. They had human lives to lead. It would be wonderful to see what they did over the years.

But Kepi had a different life. And suddenly she realized where it should be: back in the north, at the site of the great pyramid. She could watch over the workers there. She could see an accident before it happened and make everyone get to safety. She could protect the pharaoh's people even if he didn't. Ha! Everything was working out—not the way she had hoped, but better, really. She could do good things forever and ever and ever.

She flew back to the roof of her human family's home, where her new family waited for her.

AUTHOR'S NOTE

Where did fairies come from?

Pan claimed fairies were born from the first baby's first laugh. But, in Tinker Bell's infamous words, Peter was a "silly ass."

Laughter is important, no doubt about it. But fairies are linked to many things beyond happiness—scary things, wicked things, sad things, mysterious things.

Some believe they are the spirits of nature, embodied in hills, lakes, the sun, a flower's delicate perfume—that is, the basic elements of earth, water, fire, and air. Some say they were spawned on magical islands under the oceans, on the high seas, even in the skies.

They are legendary creatures, often linked to religious beliefs. So the question of where they come from is one to take seriously.

Fairies first appear in recorded history in ancient Egypt. That's why I chose to set my story there. The English word *fairy*, however, has its origin in the Latin word *fata*, which is the name of a goddess of fate (the Latin word for fate is *fatum*). That original sense of what the word meant led me to create a story in which Kepi's experiences and her relationships to the various gods inexorably lead her to her final choice of becoming a fairy; this choice is truly her fate. It is a nice coincidence, however, that two ancient Egyptian words—*nefer*, "beauty," and *meri*, "beloved"— can be blended to form *feri*, which sounds the same as *fairy*.

POSTSCRIPT ON HISTORY

This story takes place during the Fourth Dynasty of the Old Kingdom of ancient Egypt, approximately in the year 2530 BCE. Egypt had a developed civilization as early as 3000 BCE, and it continued for millennia. Much of what you might read about ancient Egypt is true of a particular time period only, not of the entire history. I have tried hard to stay true to the Egypt of the time of this story.

The sayings of Kepi's father come from inscriptions on ancient temple walls.

The gods and goddesses of Egypt are known to many people today by the Greek versions of their names. Likewise, ancient cities are known by their Greek or Arabic names. But the Greek influence on Egypt arrived much later than this story, and the Arabic influence was even later. For that reason, I have returned to the ancient Egyptian names when I could find them, and to Coptic (a later stage of Egyptian) names when I couldn't find earlier ones. The reader can use the glossary that follows to check on the identities of gods, goddesses, and place names.

I haven't been entirely consistent in this language choice, however. The ancients called their country Kimi, not Egypt. And they called their ruler *nesw-bit*, not pharaoh. I used the familiar names, however, in the hope that this would help readers keep in mind whatever they might already know about the country and use that to envision the story.

Gods and goddesses appear in Kepi's adventure repeatedly. They whisper to her, they reveal themselves to her in animal form, they protect her—sometimes with destructive results—and, ultimately, they insist that her life cannot continue on its original path, since she offended them by entering the temple and by eating the food set out for the goddess Sekhmet. When we finally see gods and goddesses interacting with each other in the dark cellar below the temple floor, they squabble. In her anger, the goddess Sekhmet talks badly about other gods, calling the god Horus bossy and the god Set untrustworthy—claims we can easily believe, given what we've seen of the gods in Kepi's story. The god Sobek, in the form of a crocodile, and the god Set, in the form of a hippo, killed men of the crew rather than merely frightening them into changing their behavior. These acts would make one think the gods had little regard for human life. Only Hathor seems just and loving in her interactions with humans. The array of gods and goddesses presented in this story, then, does little to inspire confidence. Yet the ancient Egyptians believed in such gods.

While the general role of the gods and goddesses changed over the long period of ancient Egypt's history, and while the individual personalities attributed to particular gods and goddesses varied over this period, there's no doubt that the ancients developed and observed a wide range of strict rituals in their daily lives because of the hope and, indeed, the fear that deities could be watching them at any moment. Ancient life must have felt chaotic and unreliable. One moment parents were able to work hard and provide for their family, the next day one or both sustained such a disabling injury that their lives and the lives of their loved ones were no longer secure. One moment a person was paddling in ease down the river, and the next a sandstorm came and tossed him away, ultimately drowning him. The roars of lions, whoops of hyenas, and howls of jackals sounded in the night. Yet dawn was often a mystical misty green, day saw skies teeming with happy pelicans and rivers crowded with many kinds of fish, and at sunset the sand and limestone cliffs sometimes dazzled red and white. All these goods and evils, all these gifts and miseries, all of them came from the gods and goddesses. So of course the deities themselves had to be imperfect; their imperfections helped to account for an otherwise bewildering world.

I consulted dozens of books while I was doing the research for this story. One that covers the vast span of ancient Egyptian history and fully explains the ways the gods and goddesses wove their way through all aspects of everyday life, from medicine to law, from birth to death, is Rosalie David's *Religion and Magic in Ancient Egypt* (New York: Penguin, 2003). A very fine overview of the gods and goddesses, including many minor ones and ones borrowed from other ancient cultures, which nicely focuses on indigenous Egyptian beliefs (rather than beliefs imported later from Greece or Rome) is George Hart's *A Dictionary of Egyptian Gods and Goddesses* (London: Routledge, 1986). For those interested in reading more about the pyramids and Egyptian archaeology in general, a very fine book is Kathryn Bard's *An Introduction to the Archaeology of Ancient Egypt* (Malden, Mass.: Blackwell, 2007). For many illustrations of Egyptian art, from wall carvings to etchings on amulets, with rich discussions, see Gay Robins's *The Art of Ancient Egypt* (rev. ed., Cambridge, Mass.: Harvard University Press, 2008). For an overview of history and a geographical tour of ancient sites, with photos, beautiful illustrations, and frequent maps (this is truly armchair travel), I recommend John Baines and Jaromir Malek's *Cultural Atlas of Ancient Egypt* (rev. ed., New York: Checkmark, 2000). A fine book on the literature of ancient Egypt (although most of the material in it comes from periods after the period in which Kepi's story is set) is William Kelly Simpson's *The Literature of Ancient Egypt: An Anthology of Stories, Instructions, Stelae, Autobiographies, and Poetry* (3rd ed., New Haven: Yale University Press, 2003). And for readers fascinated with ancient worlds in general, there are many marvelous books out there. One I love is *Ancient Civilizations: The Illustrated Guide to Belief, Mythology, and Art* (San Diego, Calif.: Thunder Bay, 2005), edited by Greg Woolf. Another is *The Penguin Encyclopedia of*

Ancient Civilizations (New York: Penguin Books, 1989), edited by Arthur Cotterell. But I also strongly encourage you to browse the internet for photos of ancient Egyptian sites. I visited Egypt in the fall of 2010, as I was writing this book, and I found that by following up each day's tramping around with internet searches, I often reinforced the experience by gaining closer looks at or bird's-eye views of art and archaeological sites. Further, sometimes sites are closed to the public (either in general or at the specific moment you want to visit them), but photos on the internet can allow access.

One final word: While much research goes into historical fiction, in the end I am simply a writer of fiction, not an authority on Egyptian history. So when my sources disagreed on something, I was unable to make a scholarly judgment. I have not spent decades doing archaeological research; instead, I have worked primarily from secondary sources, although I have had the privilege of actually walking through many ancient sites. Therefore, in situations of controversy, I went with the option that helped me to create the best story I could. That's the point of fiction, after all. And when one book offered something unusual (such as the fact that there's evidence that some girls wore pigtails, though children in general had shaven heads), I jumped on that as an interesting detail. I try to ground my story in details so the reader is constantly feeling the time and place, which to me are as central to the story as any character. But historical fiction is just that—fiction.

GLOSSARY

Note: Most Egyptian names have multiple transliterations and a variety of transcriptions into the Roman alphabet. Only a single version for each entry is given here.

AKHU—the part of a person that becomes a shining dot in the sky after they die

BABI—baboon-headed god

DJERTY—ancient city, on the same site as the modern city of Tod

DUNAWY—winged god, often known by the Greek name Anti

HATHOR—goddess of the moon, dancing, and music

HATTIANS—ancient people of Anatolia (in Turkey)

HEKA—ram-headed god

HEM-NETJER—priest

HEM-NETJER TEPEY—high priest

HORUS—falcon-headed god

INEB HEDJ ("WHITE WALLS")—city at the Nile

delta, later known by the Greek name Memphis; the administrative capital of united Upper and Lower Egypt. It was to the south of where Cairo now stands, on the west bank.

INR-TI—ancient city, now known as the archeological site Naga el-Gherira.

KA—the part of a person that stays with the physical self after they die

KANESH—ancient name of the central eastern Anatolian town now known as Kültepe

MINOS—ancient name of the Aegean island now known as Crete

MUN-DIGAK—ancient city of what is now Afghanistan

NEKHBET—vulture-headed goddess who guards children and mothers

NEKHEB—ancient city, on the same site as the modern city of el-Kab

NEKHEN—ancient city, on the same site as the modern city of Kom el-Ahmar

NIT—goddess of war, often known by the Greek rendering Neith

NUBT—ancient city, on the same site as the modern city of Naqada

RA—sun god

SEKER—god in charge of metalworking

SEKHMET—lion-headed goddess of battle

SET—god of storms and chaos

SOBEK—crocodile-headed god

TA-SENET—ancient city, on the same site as the modern city of Esna

TEHUTI—ibis-headed god, often known by the Greek rendering Thoth

WA'EB—helper of the priest

WASET—ancient city, often known by the Greek name Thebes, and today the site of the modern city Luxor

WETJESET-HOR—ancient city, on the same site as the modern city of Edfu

YEBU—southernmost city of Egypt, on the same site as the modern city of Aswan